Sugar's Rebellion

Kayla A. Holmes

Self Published

Copyright

The characters and events portrayed in this book are fictitious. Any similarity to real persons, living or dead, is coincidental and not intended by the author.

MASTER the Art of
READING
H66082 © Highsmith LLC 2007 (12265060)
10/12

ISBN-13 (ebook): 978-1-7369679-0-4

ISBN-13 (paperback): 978-1-7369679-2-8

Cover design by: Shalease Allen and

Kayla Holmes

Printed in the United States of America

Dedication

To my Grandparents: John West Holmes, Marie Valentine-Holmes, Alice Louise Davis-Perkins, and especially, Ezekial Perkins. Grandpa Zeke, my writing journey started with you about 20 years ago when we used to make our own short stories. I am incredibly proud to now show you this one.

Epigraph

"Creativity is a combination of discipline and childlike spirit."

Robert Greene

Table of Contents

Introduction

This story was influenced by the work of slave turned freewoman Mary Prince. Prince was the first African-British woman to escape enslavement and publish a record of her experiences with the help of the Anti-Slavery Society in England. During my sophomore year of college at The University of Pennsylvania, I had the privilege of reading her autobiographical document. I was so inspired by it, that I began to write this the subsequent summer.

Thank you Mary Prince for choosing to tell your story.

Chapter 1

Eva

My mother's screams echoed in my head as I trudged behind the large wooden wagon - the hemp rope attached to the back end of it biting deeper into my wrists. Scratches were still visible on my arm from where she clung to me, unwilling to let me go. She knew I was to be sold, but I'll never forget the look of desperation on her face when the auctioneer exclaimed, "Sold to the gentleman from Jamaica!" It was as if something broke in her. She foolishly fought to keep me by her side, to keep me in Cuba. My buyer had hit her for that…

Hard.

Hard enough that she fell to the ground and her cries stopped. I was immediately led away, the stranger's rough, calloused hands covering the area where my mother's soft and gentle ones had just been. Tears burned my eyes, begging to be released, but I refused to cry in front of the strange man. I tried to be strong, to brace myself for all that would come, but I couldn't help but look back one last time. The last image I had of my mother was of her lying lifeless, like a rag doll, on the dirt road. The wooden auctionblock was her only friend as it casted shadows over her body.

Guantánamo was my home, where I was born and raised, and it took only 30 seconds for my whole life to be flipped upside down. I would never see my mother again, never hear Mistress Lily's laugh, would never gather around the fire with my sibl-

...I shivered as a cold chill traversed across the back of my neck, ripping me from my reminiscent state. The harsh sun beating down on me couldn't have caused a reaction like that and as I looked up to find the source of my discomfort, I locked eyes with Jim Clark - my new...

Owner.

His beady blue eyes pierced into me and I quickly averted my gaze. I hated the way he intently looked at me as if he expected to find something mirrored in my eyes. At first, I thought his frightening behavior would have improved as soon as we reached Jamaican soil and were away from the close quarters of the boat, but that seemed to have just been wishful thinking. I busied myself, looking everywhere else but at him.

One rock, two rocks, three rocks, four...

I'd counted to 30 by the time the hairs on my arm fell and I knew he was no longer focused on me. Rubbing away the stinging sensation within my eyes, I quickly became aware of what had drawn Mr. Clark's attention away from me. I resisted the urge to gag as the overwhelming smell of ashes, charcoal, and burnt...wood crashed into my senses. Along the right handside of the road, miles and miles of charcoal black fields occupied my line of sight. It was a stark contrast from the bright orange of the sky and the deep green of the surrounding land.

Confusion washed over me as I took in the site.

What happened here?

Only darkness emanated from the main house. If it had not been for the burnt fields, the only indication that something malicious had occurred here were the cracks spidering along the front window of the house. I glanced over to the slave driving the wagon, hoping he might clue me in.

Again, wishful thinking.

All I received was a small shake of his head. Fiddling with the hem of my shirt, I risked looking back at my new owner for an explanation, but for once, he seemed oblivious to my existence. That's when I noticed the lines beginning to form along his forehead. Hopping down from the front of the wagon, he marched towards the closest patch of scorched earth. He stalked along the edge, his eyes flicking back and forth. Eventually he stopped, kneeled, and picked up what looked to be a piece of wood. I dared to inch closer and found it was more than bark. Char was threatening to take over, but there were still faint lines etched into the middle.

"Greenwood Plantation."

Suddenly, the hairs on my arms raised and my blood turned to ice as I realized I had spoken out loud. Mr. Clark was now staring very intently at me, eyes narrowing by the second.

"How did *you* know what this said, girl?" He was still kneeling by the sign, but at my immediate silence, he quickly rose and marched my way. I spared a glance at the driver. His eyes were downcast, face turned away from me.

"I asked you a question!" Mr. Clark boomed, yanking my binds so that I was face to face with him. Strands of jet black hair fell into his face with the force. This close, I could see beads of sweat forming above his brow. The rope bit into my wrists, forcing my body to twist with Mr. Clark's hands.

Only tell him half truths.

Finding the courage to speak, I uttered, "A-a-a free colored used to come by my old plantation and my old mistress would, sh-she would allow her to teach me a f-f-few words."

Please believe me.
He doesn't need to know you can read.
He doesn't need to kno-

"So you know how to read?" Somehow his grip on the rope tightened even more.

"No Sir. I-I's not smart enough to know how to read. I-I-I can only recognize certain words Sir."

My fingers reached for the edge of my shirt as he let my hemp shackles go. Expelling the breath of air I had been holding, I tried to look to the floor, but was stopped by Mr. Clark's frighteningly soft hands on my cheek. He forced my face up and when we locked eyes, the light blue there froze me in place.

"You would do well to address me as Master...girl," he whispered.

His hot breath on my skin brought bile to my throat. As he spoke, his knuckles lightly brushed across my lips. All I wanted to do was jerk away, put space between him and I, but his gaze kept me locked in place - locked in fear. Seconds morphed into hours as I attempted to keep calm under his gaze. Thankfully, he soon grew tired of our game, releasing me from his grasp and strolling back onto the wagon.

Just like that, the moment was over.

Thank God.

As he gave the slave driving the signal to continue, he glanced back at me once more. His tongue swept across his lips as he uttered, "Hmmm, I think you'll fit in nicely on my plantation." Following the slight tug of the rope, I walked behind the wagon in silence. The seared strip of landscape overtook my vision as we left. It washed out everything and left only darkness.

What is this place…

A voice of dread within me answered: *Welcome to Montpelier Jamaica.*

Chapter 2

Eva

The enormity of the Clark plantation stopped me dead in my tracks. The white arch loomed overhead as I entered the grounds. White stones lead from the entrance arch all the way up to the main house.

No, not a house.
The shack that I shared with my mother and siblings, that was a house...this,
This is something else entirely.

Staircase, upon staircase led up to the intricate opening of the great house, the grey ironwork of the handrails provided a stark contrast to the white stone of the building. Lush and vibrant plant life encapsulated the walkway. I was captivated by the beauty of bushels and bushels of bright orange flowers, one's I had never seen before. Their petals mirrored a sunset, but the long, tongue-like stem that jutted from the center bared red and yellow specks. They were held in white pots and marked the beginning of each staircase. I had counted fifteen windows before a thundering snap forced my head away from the front of the house and towards a small, caramel skinned woman kneeling in front of a man of the same color. From my position, it looked as if they were holding hands and I risked a smile at the small act of intimacy between the two slaves. It was shocking to believe such things could occur out in the open.

Maybe these new people are like Mistresses Lily - she always treated my family with kindness.

As I drew closer, I saw that the girl was actually holding a small brush in her mud encrusted hands. Her knuckles were bleeding and cracked. The man in front of her held a long thin piece of leather, his ebony hand wrapped tightly around it. He sneered at her - the disgust in his eyes mirrored the looks I had only reserved for my new, white owner. I never imagined I would see it on the face of one who shared my situation. The smile that had just graced my face fleeted as I took in the scene. Understanding ripped through me.

"I told you to clean these stones, not take breaks! The master and mistress of the house like the outside spotless...all dirt, all grime, all things that will take away from the light of the stones are to be scrubbed away immediately! Do you understand?"

"Y-yes Joseph...I'm so sorry, the heat was a-gettin' to me and I had just stopped to catch my brea-"

WHACK.

The girl cried out as Joseph brought the whip down upon her hands once more.

"I don't care what was going on, this needs to be finished by the time night falls."

This slave named Joseph finally took note of my and Mr. Clark's presence. Locking eyes with Mr. Clark, Joseph continued his onslaught on the poor girl with renewed effort.

"And look at what you've done! Now there's blood on the stones, every fleck of it betta be gone by the time Mr. Damien comes back to check!"

Joseph stared at the girl, back at Mr. Clark, and then quickly made his exit. Risking a quick glance at Mr. Clark, I found a slight smile pressed upon his lips.

The whiteness of the architecture suddenly became overwhelming, as if it was threatening to choke me. My mind reeled everytime I tried to take in the Greathouse. The beauty stripped away as I imagined all the horrors that must occur in order to keep everything right.

You mean white.

The frown on my face deepened and Mr. Clark shifted his attention back to me.

It was never gone for too long.

"That was Joseph, he's my...somewhat of a junior overseer and works under the head slave driver Damien," Mr. Clark chuckled, "I'm pleased to see Joseph taking his responsibilities...so seriously."

Apparently, Mr. Clark was done sharing as a hard push from behind forced me to continue up the pathway. I was only able to briefly lock eyes with the girl as I was herded past. Unshed tears coated her eyes as she began to profusely scrub at the red spots now littering the pavement.

So this is my new prison.

My hand threatened to fiddle with my shirt as Mr. Clark led me up to the main house where a tall woman stood, waiting. The rose color of her dress popped against the golden-brown of her skin, light freckles danced across her cheeks. Tightly coiled locks were styled into an elegant bun. It suddenly made me very subconscious of the dirtied beige shirt and ripped brown trousers I was wearing.

Even though a slave, even though outside, her presence filled the space. The bags under her eyes didn't keep her from smiling brightly at me. The ends of my lips unconsciously curled upwards in response as my hand dropped to my side. All of the distress from earlier was blotted out by her spirit, by her energy, and I couldn't help but feel inexplicably drawn to the stranger. Upon reaching the mysterious woman, Mr. Clark abandoned his position behind me to approach her.

"Betsie, take care to show this new girl where she'll be working in the house and show her to her living quarters...you know the drill," he stated, waving a dismissive hand towards me as he entered the house.

My back straightened with his sudden departure and my eyes fell upon Betsie, whose eyes were instead downcasted towards my raw, pink wrists.

"Poor child, I'll help ya clean those up right after I show ya around this here house, gotta make sure yo' hands are ready fo' yo' work tomorra. You'll be mostly carein' to tha needs of tha mistress of tha house, but every now and then you'll help me out 'round tha kitchin'... shoot, where are my manners! My name's Betsie and yo' name child?"

I stared blankly into Ms. Betsie's face, struck by her ability to talk a mile a minute. Before I could help myself, the words were already spilling from my mouth:

"Where do you find the time to breathe?"

Silence.

My hand threatened to dart back to my shirt at the thought of offending Ms. Betsie, but she quickly shook her head as if waking from a daze and laughed. It was a full and hearty laugh, a laugh that had warmth, a laugh that one wouldn't expect to find in a place like this. Ms. Betsie's eyes were closed, and her shoulders bounced effortlessly with each chuckle...she was at ease.

"Oh my goodness, ya sure are a funny one!" She must have seen the skeptical look on my face because she followed up with, "Oh don't worry sweetheart, I'm not offended! My mama always said I had a mouth that ran at full tilt, and I always told her that was good because all the more friends I could make with it. Ha! You just caught me off guard with yo' question. Most of the new faces 'round here are either too shy or too scared to do more than nod at me."

Ms. Betsie briefly stopped to take me in, her eyes swept over me from head to toe.

"I think we are goin' to get along great you and I, but if only I knew yo' name...You never did answer my question." She smiled.

"E-e-eva, Ms. Betsie. My name is Eva Turner."

"Well Ms. Eva, why don'tcha come on inta tha house wit me and I'll help ya get acquainted."

Without waiting for my reply, Betsie quickly turned on one heel and entered the house. Despite the back and forth rhythm my hand was making along the bottom of my shirt, I couldn't help the ends of my mouth turning up once more as I followed the boisterous woman inside.

Chapter 3

Eva

The sun had set by the time Betsie had finished showing me around the house and introducing me to all the other house slaves. I learned along the way that the girl who was scrubbing the stone walkways earlier was Mary, a fellow house slave of age 14.

Only three years younger than I.

My initial impression of Ms. Betsie was also confirmed along the tour. She made what should have been a stressful and overwhelming experience somewhat bearable. The tour had begun with her doctoring my wrists. Watching her clean out and bandage my cuts had brought tears to my eyes. She had been so gentle with the damp cloth that was brushed over and around my wounds. The delicate, but firm touch she had while wrapping each wrist reminded me of home, of a time when I felt safe.

You're foolish if you think you're safe here.

Tiny dots of bright orange and yellow caught my attention as we exited the main house. Curious as to what could be going on at this time of night, I focussed in on the lights. In the distance, I noticed black bodies moving in and out of a huge structure - like ants. Billows of smoke poured out from the chimneys, creating a haze on the night sky.

"What is that house over there Ms. Betsie, the one with all the smoke?"

"Oh child, that's tha kogehus, or ya may be more familiar wit tha term boilin' house."

"Boiling house?"

Stopping and turning to face me, Ms. Betsie searched my face to see if I was feigning ignorance.

"Ya don't know what goes on in kogehus? Have ya ever been on a suga' plantation before?"

Heat rose to my cheeks as I refused to look Ms. Betsie in the eye. Thankful that the darkness of nightfall hid most of my embarrassment, I quickly answered her. "Uh, n-no ma'am, I've n-never been on a sugar plantation before, only heard whispers...m-my last owner, Mistress Lilly, had a small tobacco plantation. It was very different from here, n-nothing along this scale."

My eyes were still downcast when a hand gently grabbed mine. Ms. Betsie had my hands in a tight grip. She locked eyes with me before speaking. The light brown of them somehow glowed in the moonlight.

"Not to worry sweetheart, I'll teach ya everythin' ya need to know, startin' wit that there building." She assured, releasing my hands. The once soothing night air was now a bit too chilly.

"That kogehus is where all tha liquid suga is heated. It goes through many boilin' stages before becomin' crystallized at tha end of tha whole process."

Turning away from the boiling house - *the kogehus* - Ms. Betsie gestured towards the path in front of us.

"Now come on, we can walk and talk about the rest...I'd like to make it back to tha quarters before it gets too late." With that, she turned on her heel, leading me further and further away from Mr. and Mrs. Clark's home.

Ms. Betsie pointed out everything she could think of as we made the trek towards the slave village. This being my first time on a sugar plantation, there was quite a lot to point out. From the tall, cylindrical sugar mill, to the smaller curing building adjacent to the kogehus, and the large cistern that was apparently used to collect rainwater for sugar production. The sugar cane stretched out in front of the slave village. It made an eerily tall barrier between us and the Great House. The night air breezed through the sugar cane stalks, providing Ms. Betsie and I with a strange kind of music as we walked. Soon the melody changed, natural sounds traded in for soft, lilty notes. The tune was sweet, happy, and every few beats there was a slight change to the pattern of notes. There seemed to be no rhyme or reason.

"What is that, it's beautiful," I wistfully asked, "Is that always playing at night around here?"

"Oh, that's George. He made a makeshift banjo years ago out of a leftover gord we had…"

I smiled in the direction of the music, letting the calming melody fill my senses.

"...and to answer yo' otha question, no, he...he doesn't play every night."

A deep sigh escaped Ms. Betsie's lips as she finished speaking, compelling me to really focus on her. Her back was turned to me.

"Ms. Betsie?" I whispered.

For the first time she refused to look my way, but I could still make out the slight downturn of her lips.

"George plays that there tune to signal a successful change in shifts without any...any accidents - so no, unfortunately he doesn't get to play that melody everyday."

She finally turned to look at me and smiled, but the light of it failed to reach her eyes. Silence passed between us until a low chuckle escaped Ms. Betsie's mouth.

"Well sometimes ole' George *will* play on special occasions, and almost every Sunday too!"

"What happens on Sundays tha-"

"Oh well we get most Sundays off sweetie! See it's a time fo' us to come together. Some of us are able to go to tha market and trade, and others may tend to personal gardens that you can find further back behind tha slave houses. Tha plots aren't much, not a lot of good soil and too many rocks, but I *was* able to get a pretty decent amount of sweet potatoes and plantains last year - not to braff.[1] We'll see about ya finding a plot of yo' own in tha mornin'... oh shoot, there I go assumin' again! Do ya even want to garden child?"

My eyes closed and my mind drifted back to a time when I was half my size. My mom knelt by a small mound of dirt, a series of bright green leaves jutted from the ground between her knees. Her fingers swept over the plant leaves and a crazy grin lit her face. She looked back at me, gesturing for me to come feel. I abandoned my watering can and knelt down beside my mother. Her large hands engulfed mine as they led them over the fuzzy leaves of the plant. Small creases in

---

[1] "Braff" - patois for "showing off"

the corners of her eyes formed as we grinned at each other.

"Look at our first plant grow," my mother said, "I'm so so proud."

When my eyes opened, I was met with a concerned look from Ms. Betsie. She moved closer to me and repeated herself.

"Eva, are ya okay? Do ya want a plot? If all this is too much, ya just say tha word and I'll stop tal-"

"No, no you're fine. I'd actually love a gardening plot, it'd remind me of home. Thanks Ms. Betsie..." She started to turn away. "...but you know you don't have to do all this for me. Be nice to me and all that, I could find a plot on my own."

"Oh don't be silly child! A lot of us, not every slave on this here plantation, but a lot of us are like family and we take care of each otha as much as possible...and findin' ya a plot is really no trouble at all.

It'll be easy, seein' as to how I know all tha right people." Ms. Betsie winked in my direction. " Findin' a plot would have most likely taken ya quite a while due to how ya don't know too many folks 'round here just yet."

From her tone, I knew she was teasing. But, she was also right. So, I just humbly smiled and uttered, "thanks." Ms. Betsie hummed a sound of approval before continuing on.

George's music wasn't the only sign of our arrival to the slave quarters. As we got closer and closer to where I would be sleeping, the smell of animal - *or possibly human* - waste hit me like a ton of bricks. Tears began to form at the corners of my eyes and a small gagging sound slipped out. Noticing my discomfort, Betsie slowed.

"Sorry 'bout tha smell sweetheart," she uttered in a tone I had not heard before.

For the second time tonight, her demeanor lost its airiness as she looked off to her left towards the sugar cane fields.

"It's an unfortunate hazard of workin' here."

Following her gaze, my eyes settled on women walking towards the cane fields. Their skin was dark as night, and large wooden buckets sat atop their heads. A chunky, yet loose brown substance leaked from the sides and occasionally spilled over the top. The reality of what was transpiring knocked the air from my lungs and a sharp sound pushed past my lips as if I had been hit in the stomach. My teeth groaned in protest as I clamped my mouth shut. Resisting the urge to vomit, I grabbed onto Betsie as we carried on to my quarters.

I struggled to keep up as Ms. Betsie pointed out one thing after another. There was so much to take in, so much to remember, and the trauma of the day caused my thoughts to jumble. I tried my best to remain focused, solely because of

Ms. Betsie. She had gone above and beyond trying to help and guide me. The sun had long set, but her favor never dimmed. No matter how many questions flowed past my filter, Ms. Betsie answered every one to the best of her ability. Her honesty and sincerity made my heart pound sporadically and caused my throat to constrict. I owed it to her to at least try and retain half of what was being shown to me.

Along the way, Ms. Betsie identified the cooking house for slaves. It sat perched in a hollowed out piece of land a good distance from the seemingly endless rows of slave cabins.

"To prevent fires"

"What?" I responded, shaking my head slightly.

"I saw ya lookin', the cookin' house is so far from tha quarters to prevent fires. Masta Clark didn't want us slaves dyin' unnecessarily when there is so much work to be done."

Looking out the corner of my eye, I gave Ms. Betsie my best smirk, "How thoughtful."

Ms. Betsie snorted softly, "My sentiments exactly."

After two rows of slave houses passed by, Ms. Betsie stopped and gestured towards a cabin with a wooden workbench out front, both official and makeshift tools littered the top of it.

"Now right here," Ms. Betsie started, "that's where tha horse handler lives! He tends to tha Masta's horses and just so happens to also be good wit his hands. He's in charge of a lot of tha fixin' 'round here and a little bit up at tha main house. So if ya eva need anythin' fixed, made, or just wanna talk, don't hesitate to go to him ya hear."

Quickly nodding in agreement, I turned and caught a glimpse of something metal.

"What's that thing over there?"

Leaving Betsie, I drifted to the right side of the horse handler's house where there was a medium sized clearing with what looked to be a pig trough in the center of it. Looking further down the row of cabins, I spotted several clearings sporadically placed throughout. Within each clearing, moonlight caught and bounced off of what I assumed were also troughs.

"Oh troughs like that one are all throughout tha slave quarters. The Masta of tha house sometimes allows Damien to put leftovers from their diners in tha troughs for us to eat."

Turning around, I found Ms. Betise with her lips pressed into a thin line, her eyes narrowed in on the metal bin.

"Our weekly rations aren't enough fo' some, so it can get pretty crazy 'round here when tha Masta decides to...*feed tha dogs.*" The last part she spat, as if the words were like poison on her lips.

Walking back towards her, it was my turn to try and comfort Ms. Betsie as I gently laid a hand on her shoulder. Even through the material of her dress, her skin was hot to the touch and a fire burned in her eyes. Attempting to get her mind off of the feeders, my next question focused on something slightly different.

"So this Damien, he's the overseer? I only ask because I haven't seen him yet?"

Rather than relax, Betsie's eyes sharpened. Something different sparked in her gaze, and her hand shot up to grab the one I had placed on her shoulder.

"God," she whispered heatedly, "pray ya neva meet him child. Do everythin' ya can to stay outta Damien's path."

Turning back around to face the sugar cane once more, Ms. Betsie gestured past them towards two houses that sat to the left of the Great House.

"Tha larger one," Ms. Betsie continued, "that there is Damien's house. And tha otha one right there…" she pointed to a hut smaller than Damien's house, but much larger than anything I had seen within the slave quarters. It sat only a handful of paces away from Damien's house. "Tha slave Joseph, Damien's right hand man, and his family live there."

My thoughts flashed back to the scene of Joseph punishing Mary earlier. Instinctively, one of my hands closed into a fist, while the other simultaneously reached for the hem of my shirt.

"Yeah, I've had the pleasure of meeting Joseph already."

"Not a fan?" Betsie questioned.

A snort was all that I could muster in reply as Bestie gestured ahead of me and led me deeper into the rows of slave houses.

"Ya know...our condition has a funny way of makin' tha nicest people do sum of tha most vile things," she responded as she walked past.

Hesitating, I looked back at the grandeur of Joseph's house - Ms. Betsie's words echoed in my head.

One row ahead and four houses to the right of the mystery horse trainer's, Betsie eventually stopped in front of a sad, slightly leaning shack.

My new home.

Even though I had walked past several of them, seeing one up close was still shocking. The rectangular structure was made from wood. Plantain leaves closed in the hut, creating the roof. The sides of the hut had dozens of little notches etched deep into the outer walls. The door protested as I pushed my way through it.

Inside is no better.

A square table was set up against the furthest wall and to the left of the door, a thin mat laid atop the dirt floor. A dress, a new set of trousers, a linen shirt, and two strips of cloth Betsie called "bandanas" sat folded on the small table.

"You can use tha longer bandana as a skirt and tha otha fo' tyin' yo' hair up... that one there really comes in handy on tha extremely hot days," she quickly added as I stroked my hand over the fabric, taking in the rest of the room.

It wasn't necessarily the conditions of the hut that concerned me, but more so how deserted it felt. It was dark, empty, and cold - nothing like the home I had back in Cuba. We may not have had much, but my mother, siblings, and I made sure our home was warm and lively, full of whatever joy we could muster. All of the events from the past couple of days suddenly came flooding past my defenses. Despair made my knees go weak, and I couldn't help it as my hand reached for the end of my shirt. The emotional cap I had set in place shattered into a million pieces.

The loss of everything I had ever known, the long and uneasy journey, and this new place, it all threatened to overtake me. I could feel myself drowning and I failed to see the light guiding me back to the water's surface.

A soft hand on my shoulder and a warm presence at my back froze me in place. I hadn't even realized I was shaking until Betsie's hand anchored me in place. Her silence spoke volumes. My eyes burned with unshed tears and my breath ran jagged as I struggled to release the pressure in my chest. Betsie gently turned me to face her and pulled me into her embrace. My brain screamed at me to pull it together and let her go - but I couldn't.

What are you doing Eva!

The weight of what I was about to admit spread an asphyxiating feeling throughout my body and my hand clenched around another's clothing for once. For the first time since leaving Cuban soil, I felt comfortable and at peace in Betsie's arms. We had only known each other for an afternoon, but I could feel myself getting attached. I was relying on her strength and this revelation scared me because I knew all too well the dangers that could arise from slaves letting people get past their walls. My family, my mother and siblings, used to be the only ones I'd ever let in. Naivety allowed me to think my family could never be the ones to cause me pain, but their absence burned a hole in my chest.

In a place like this, reliance will lead to nothing but heartache and pain.

Despite my better judgment and my inner turmoil, I held on to Betsie as if she were my only lifeline.

"Why don'tcha come by my hut befo' gettin' settled," Betsie whispered in a quiet voice, "there's someone I want ya to meet."

Chapter 4

Eva

The cool night air helped settle me as we left my shack. Betsie lived three huts down. Her's was about the same size as mine, but had a little square opening to the right of the door and a carving of a sun etched deep into the wood above it. The little opening was no bigger than a sheet of paper. A candle in that makeshift window was the only hint to the presence of someone inside. Betsie stepped back, allowing me to go first. Opening the door, I moved to cross the threshold, but met a solid, rigid form. Broad shoulders loomed over me as I came face to face with a golden-brown back littered with grey and black lines. The harsh pattern they made was mesmerizing. I would have starred longer, if the heat rising in my cheeks hadn't gotten the best of me. Expecting anger, my head fell towards the floor, but words never came. Instead, a calloused hand pressed lightly on my chin, forcing my head back up. His right cheek pulled back, revealing a dimple. The smirk was borderline menacing, but the onyx eyes that stared back into mine showed no indication of malice. The warmth that I found within them caused familiarity to spread through me.

"Eva Turner," Betsie snickered behind me, "meet my son Jacob. Jacob this is Eva. She's new 'roun-"

"I can see that mama," he interrupted, smirking in his mother's direction.

Betsie glared daggers at her son. Most people would have been shut-down by the look, it was so cold, but Jacob only grinned harder in response.

"As I **was** sayin', she's not from 'round here. She'll be workin' with Mistress Clark up in tha main house. Eva," her focus flipped to me as she made her way to Jacob, stretching up to place a hand on his shoulder, "my son here is tha plantation handyman and takes care of all tha horses."

With that, she shot a smug smile my way. Mirth danced in her eyes as she watched understanding wash over my face.

"You-you're the horse handler and the handyman...the one who lives near me?"

I wasn't really addressing the question to anyone specifically, but a delighted Betsie didn't even give Jacob a chance to respond as she clasped her hands together.

"Yep, he's one and tha same! How nice it is that you two are gonna be so close!"

Not even stopping to breath, Betsie rolled on.

"It's actually perfect because I want ya to keep an eye out fo' her as much as possible Jacob...make sure she doesn't get in to too much trouble 'round here. She's new to this type of plantation so I want her to have as much support as we can give her!"

"Not sure I should be the one trying to keep her outta trouble," he responded as his hand reached out between us.

I couldn't help the upturn of my lips at what I thought was a joke. Seeing my amusement, Jacob finally gave me a full fledged smile. When his teeth showed, it was hard to miss his relation to his mother. Betsie on the other hand glared at her son, her lips pursed together. The look she gave him rivaled anything my mother threw at me. I swore I could hear her teeth grind, but Jacob seemed unbothered as my hand went out to meet his.

"Nice to meet you Jacob. I hope I can rely on you," I joked.

Despite his earlier jesting, he suddenly grew serious. His hand tightened slightly around mine and I was shocked to see his eyes harden into an even darker shade.

Black as night

Those dark abysses ensnared me as his next words came out steady and strong. "Don't worry Eva, I'll look out for you."

I believed every word

Chapter 5

Eva

Betsie whipped up a meal of sweet potato and maize for us to eat. Watching Betsie work made it clear why she was the plantation's head cook. She didn't have to give all of her attention to cooking, she would talk and laugh without even glancing down at the pot. It was as if her hands knew exactly what to do without the help of her eyes. I'd never seen anything like it. In what seemed like no time, Betsie had three bowls of food laid out before Jacob and I. We had migrated to the cooking house and the walk over had worked up an even bigger appetite within us. Jacob dug right in, his wooden spoon scraping along the side of the calabash bowl.

"Manners boy," Betsie scolded as her hand struck the back of Jacob's head, eliciting a look from him. Despite his protest, he straightened up.

Watching the banter between the two helped take my mind off of everything to come. It almost felt normal, eating with people again.

"So Eva," Jacob interrupted my thoughts, "ma said you were new to this type of plantation - what'd your Master grow if not sugar?"

"There was no man of the house," I sharply corrected. Softening my tone with a quick '*ahem*', I quickly added, " there was only a Mistress, Mistress Lily, and she owned a small tobacco plantation."

"Ta-tobacco," Betsie parsed out, "what's that, I've never heard of tha crop?"

I jumped at the opportunity to explain - elated that for once, I wasn't the one in the dark.

"It's a plant that has this thick, hairy stem and these big leaves that are shaped almost like elongated circles. It's mostly used for smoking and sometimes, white, red, or the prettiest pink flowers bloom from the plants. The plants were actually quite beautiful, but that's coming from the perspective of someone who didn't have to pick the tobacco leaves. I mostly helped Mistress Lily with the gardening and any other housework that needed to be done."

When my mouth finally closed, not one ounce of moisture was left on my tongue.

Reaching for the cup shaped gourd, I took a sip of water and spared a look across the table. Jacob was looking at me intently, mulling over my words, while Betsie just nodded.

"Good, good, tha house work ya did ova' at yo' ol' plantation will help ya complete yo' duties as Mistress Clark's handmaid. And ya said a woman ran tha plantation? Huh, well I'll be, neva would have thought such a thing was possible!"

A hearty laugh followed Betsie's words.

I glanced at Jacob, who had long been quiet. Little lines were forming at the corners of his mouth and he stared right through me as darkness returned to his eyes. When he finally opened his mouth to speak, it wasn't an expected response.

"See ma," he started, "there are some people out there breaking these clear cut norms you seem to believe in."

"Oh kibba yuh mouth[2] boy, not this nonsense again," Betsie muttered as her eyes closed and her fingers pressed against her temples.

"It's not nonsense ma, when are you going to see that!" Jacob yelled, banging his spoon against the table.

"Put clothes pon yuh argument![3] I'm not gonna say this again, hush boy...before tha wrong ears hear ya!"

---

[2] "Kibba yuh mouth" - patois for "shut-up"
[3] "Put clothes pon yuh argument" - patois for "mind what you're saying" or "show some respect while speaking to me"

My head jumped from person to person as they bickered. It was as if the both of them had forgotten I was there. Jacob's hands had released his spoon and were now squeezed into fists. He and his mother were locked in a stare down. I could see the slow burning anger beneath both of the surfaces of their skin.

Hot tempers must run in the family.

Curiosity burned to the forefront of my mouth, forcing me to break the silence.

"I'm confused, what 'nonsense' are we talking about?"

It looked as if they had been electrocuted, the way their heads snapped towards me, finally remembering they weren't actually alone. I only captured Betsie's attention for a moment before she immediately returned her gaze upon Jacob. His eyes were instead still locked on me, determination etched into the set of his jaw.

"Don't ya dare -" Betsie started, but Jacob quickly cut her off.

"I was just reminding my mother that there could be more to life than this current existence."

Despite still being unsure of what he was talking about, I sat up straighter and leaned forward.

"Specifically," he continued, "I'm talking about the maroon communities. Places, Eva, where we could live free -"

"Supposedly," Betsie quickly interjected. Her tone was cold and sharp, as she eyed the door. But Jacob's passion wasn't so easily snuffed.

"We would be free Eva! Free from masters and their degrading control. We would rule our own lives, set our own destinies." His words came out in a blur as excitement took over. His eyes were still locked with mine. The blackness that had just resided there was now replaced by a warm and liquidy dark brown.

Like a cocoa bean - I mused, remembering the time I got to hold one as a child.

"Really?" My breath came out in a whisper.

Common sense was telling me to be wary of such information. But despite what my head thought was right, something warm blossomed deep within me. Betsie must have seen it, for she quickly interjected.

"Why are ya feedin' dis here girl's head wit fairytales, what proof do ya have?"

"Haven't you heard of Cudjoe, they say he's leading the maroon community closest to us, he's persuading slaves to resist! I've heard stories of these marooners looting the plantations they used to work, freeing slaves along the way, and even burning fields...There ARE slaves out there fighting back and making it difficult for the English men to stay here."

I froze at the mention of burning fields.

The Greenwood Plantation.

"Did you say they're burning crops?" I responded.

"Oh sweetheart don't be frightened by Jacob's words, he doesn't know what he's talkin' 'bout. Like he said, they're just stories."

My head angled to the side and my eyes narrowed as I put two and two together.

"I don't think she's scarred ma," Jacob hesitated for a moment, watching me intently, "She's seen something. What was it Eva, what did you see?"

"I don't know exactly, but I might have seen evidence of the burning fields thing you were just talking about. On my way to this here plantation, Mr. Clark and I came upon a deserted piece of land...the Greenwood Plantation I believe it was called."

At its mention, Betsie and Jacob shared a look.

"A-all the fields, what I'm assuming used t-t-to be sugar cane, the-they were burnt to a crisp. Black fields was all I could s-see for miles..." Returning from the memory, I blinked a couple of times and met Jacob's stare. Surprisingly, a smirk was now plastered on his face.

"...Was that an act of resistance?" I questioned.

"I believe it was Eva," Jacob answered, "See ma, there's your evidence right there! It's no longer just me, Eva has witnessed some of the marooners' actions. The sugar workers are rebelling - and at the Greenwood Plantation no less...that's not even that far from here!"

"*Tap*[4] - just stop, please!" One of Betsie's hands wrapped tightly around Jacob's bicep. Her voice faltered as she tried to continue, "And what if this escape plan of yours fails huh? Have ya even thought of that, of what it would do to me! You of all people know tha risks of disobedience and I wouldn't be able to survive anythin' happenin' to you again...not - not again."

Her hand shook as she released him and turned away. A single tear fell from her right eye. Before I could think about it, my hand shot out to grab hers, trying to give a fraction of the strength she had recently given me.

"Mother."

Jacob reached out to try and place a hand on her shoulder, but Betsie shrugged in on herself and he let his arm fall.

"Mother," he started again, "I'm fine...and I'm willing to do whatever it

---

[4] Tap - Patois for "stop"

takes to get us out of here. Can't you at least understand that."

He spoke with such confidence that had I not been looking at him, I would have believed his words. However the sight of his own trembling hand dashing behind his back indicated that things weren't exactly "fine." Closing my eyes, I squeezed Betsie's hand tighter as all the pieces came together. The image of Jacob's back and the horrorshow of grey and black lines that lived there pushed to the forefront of my mind. No matter how close I believed to have become with Ms. Betsie, I knew this was a time for me to be quiet. After an agonizingly slow minute, Betsie had composed herself enough to release my hand and face her son again.

"I'm sorry son, but I just don't see tha appeal nor tha need to 'rouse up sparks of hope within tha good people here - especially when there's no guarantee. We are slaves, and I hate to say it, but we probably gon' die slaves. To allow us to believe we can be anythin' else, it...it's foolish and unwise. That kind of mentality could put people in unnecessary danger."

Jacob's shoulders finally caved in as he stood from the table.

"A tiny spark of hope ma, can turn into a roaring flame."

He held Betsie's gaze one last time, took a deep breath, and then silently disappeared into the night.

Chapter 6

Eva

I helped Betsie clean up the mess from dinner, but after the abrupt end to the evening, there wasn't really much more for Betsie and I to discuss. Silence passed between us as she accompanied me back to my hut. My brain rattled as I searched for the right words…

Scratch that.

...any words to try and bring back the light and easy atmosphere from before. No matter what I came up with though, by the time my mouth opened, the words just didn't seem to fit anymore. As we walked, I struggled to find the geniality I had come to associate with Betsie. Her posture was so rigid, her head was cocked up in defiance. Resigning myself to the tense quiet, my fingertips swept mindlessly across the bottom of my shirt.

One step, two steps, three steps, four…

Surprisingly, not even counting could deter my anxiety.

By the time we reached my hut, Betsie had thawed enough to bid me goodnight with a fierce hug and a light kiss on the cheek. She smiled at me, the light of it not fully reaching her eyes, before leaving with a wave and a shout over her shoulder.

"Remember we ought to be ready for chores in a few hours."

For a while, I just stood at the entrance of the hut, staring after Betsie. I felt a suffocating urge to call after her, dreading the loneliness that was going to overtake me. My breath came out in short bursts as my hand left my shirt and reached for the door. In the brief time it took for me to push the creaking Blue Mahoe door open, a dull ache suddenly began working its way up my legs. Having neither the energy, nor the desire to explore my new home, I headed straight for the shadowed silhouette of my mat. The outline of a small sheet caught my attention as I sank onto the floor. Even without the sun lighting up the sky, I could still feel the thickness of heat in the air. My limbs grew heavy as I laid back, face up, on the mat. Despite the warmth, I couldn't help the chill that ran down my spine. Closing my eyes, I threw the sheet over my legs and attempted to get comfortable.

Laying in the darkness of my hut, I returned to the hem of my shirt, flicking it back and forth. The cool, solid ground pressed into my back.

What would tomorrow be like - working for this Mistress Clark?

Maybe she'll be like Mistress Lily - a saint of a lady known to treat her house slaves like family…

My stomach dragged and clenched.

You know that's not what's going to happen - Don't be foolish Eva.

My mind raced with all the possibilities of how tomorrow could go. I had just started to believe peace would escape me when squeals from the neighboring pig pens eventually drowned out all other thoughts, lulling me to sleep.

Chapter 7

Eva

I awoke to the softest rays of light breaking in under my door, the sound of my neighbors' quiet laughter could be heard as they prepared for the day. Rising, I quickly joined in on the morning commotion, washing in the murky water that apparently filled the troughs when food was absent. My trembling hands failed to press out the wrinkles in the dress I had chosen to throw on. Jacob was long gone by the time I was done, but Betsie came to walk the long path back up to the main house with me. She was a few paces ahead and was jabbering on about something important most likely, but for once I had no control over my body's ability to focus. Betsie's voice faded to a dull hum in my mind until we reached the overwhelming presence of the main house's steps. A faint red stain could still be seen at the base of the first set of stairs.

The sun sat low in the sky by the time we made it to the main house. Betsie left me in the foyer with an assembly of women who would be my fellow house workers. She only had time to briefly introduce me to some faces before zipping over to the kitchen to begin making breakfast for the Clarks and Damien. One of the faces present happened to be Mary's, her hands were bandaged in white cloth, her face solum. I offered a smile in her direction and was pleasantly surprised to receive a shier version as I settled between her and another woman named Harriet. With Betsie's departure, I attempted to draw strength from all the other women in the room. An act that almost worked while we huddled together, whispering softly as we waited for our orders. My shoulders eventually sagged, my chest loosened, and I relished in the comfort it brought me to talk aimlessly with other women. I almost forgot where I was…

Almost.

That brief moment of calm ended as soon as Mistress Clark, a tall, thin woman, entered the room. Her light yellow hair was pulled tightly back into a bun. Coming from deep within the house, she tore through our huddle, immediately set her eyes upon me, and smiled. It didn't illicite the same comforting response as Betsie's. The way all the other workers averted their gaze when she burst in caused alarm to build at the base of my neck. With a snap of her finger, I was drawn to the front.

The scene looked like a funeral procession.

As I inched closer to her, the head of every woman I passed was bowed low to the floor. Stopping in front of her, a slender finger reached out to angle my head up for inspection. Peering down at me through squinted eyes, her gaze unnerved me in a way similar to her husband...

but...

but, there was something peculiar about the way her gaze leisurely slid over me. There was an edge to it.

The reasoning behind it, I had yet to figure out.

A simple nod dismissed me back to my position between Mary and Harriet. Not even a glance was spared in my direction. The other women still had their heads bowed and not a sound had been uttered. Mistress Clark addressed each of her house workers by name and one by one, I watched as duties were given out.

"Harriet, you are with Betsie for today. In addition to the preparation of food, I expect you to aid her at all meal services. In between, you will help her tend to the day's wounded."

"Mary, you are responsible for the maintenance of the kitchen gardens - I don't want a repeat of what happened yesterday…"

At the mention of her beating, I felt Mary flinch next to me. My hand threatened to reach out to her, but with the

Mistress focused in on our direction, I dared not move.

"Once the gardens are tended to and all the produce has been washed and stored," Mistress Clark continued, "you Mary will tend to the Master's laundry. In addition to the usual washing, there are some clothes of his that need mending as well."

"For you Katy, I have made a list of all the things we need from the market downtown. Take Tess with you and make sure we get everything listed. Once you have returned, you both will aid Mary."

On and on Mistress Clark went and as soon as each woman was armed with the day's tasks, they scattered like roaches - leaving me alone with the Mistress.

"You," She turned to address me, "will be my new helper. You will pick out my clothes, help me dress, wash them, and sometimes aid Betsie in the preparation of my food. There may be some days when I ask you to perform duties outside of those just listed. Do you understand?"

My simple nod seemed to be satisfactory enough as she turned and stepped deeper into the house. As soon as she was out of earshot, a breath of air finally eased past my lips. I fought the itch in my hand as I scurried after her.

Chapter 8

Eva

My day was a whirlwind of non-stop activity - from dusting, to sweeping, to arranging, to washing…

My final task of the day

The washroom was a small area in the cellar beneath the main house. Brick and dirt were my walls, and stone my floor - stone that made your knees go numb as you knelt beside the basins. My back screamed in protest as I stretched. I had been bent over a basin for what felt like the past 4 hours. Wringing the water from a cloth and wiping my hands across the folds of my dress, I glanced down at my now semi-dry hands. Blotchy red spots littered them, and the ends of my fingers were shriveled into an alien pattern. Rubbing my hands against my dress once more, I attempted to press the creases out. My throat constricted when I raised my hands and still found lines on my fingertips. I moved to dry my hands again when a light tap on my shoulder caused me to look up. Mary, the only other company I had while washing, reached out to still my now shaking hands.

"Don't worry," she spoke so quietly, I would have missed it had I not been staring right at her, "there's nothing wrong with your hands. That wrinkling happens whenever our hands are in water for a long time. In time, it'll disappear."

Without waiting for a response, Mary released my hands and shuffled over to her basin. Once back to her pile of clothes, she quickly surveyed the room, glancing over her shoulder towards the door. Despite being the only two in the room, I had caught Mary doing that several times while down here. With each passing second, she grew more jittery and nervous. Deciding to leave Mary to her thoughts, I rocked up into a standing position. I was about to leave when the heavy thuds of someone descending the stairs stopped me short. Whipping around, I focused on the steps, anxious to see who was coming. Out the corner of my eye, I saw Mary flinch. But unlike me, she didn't turn around. The thuds only proceeded to make her work faster, the brush in her hand becoming a blur as she scrubbed at the trousers in her basin. Inching towards the steps, I attempted to get a better look and was relieved to see a familiar face.

"Harriet? What are you doing down here? Shouldn't you be busy making dinner with Betsie?" I spoke, as the woman reached the final step.

"Ha," she snorted as she caught her breath, leaning up against the railing.

"You right, I should be, but I was sent to deliver a message. Are you finished with the Mistress' laundry?"

"Yes, it's finished. I was actually just about to head out, Mrs. Clark told me I was done after this."

"Sorry to keep you from leavin' sweetie, but Mistress Clark wants to see you up in her quarters before you go. You know the way?"

"Yes," I breathed as my shoulders sagged inwards, "I do."

After making it up four flights of stairs, I knocked on the Mistress' door. My hands fidgeted with themselves as I failed to slow my breathing. I heard a faint "*enter*" from within and hesitantly pushed my way into the room. Mrs. Clark sat on the bed, waiting for me. The bed was framed by four oak posts. A vanity, dresser, couch, and a small table with chairs completed the room. When Mrs. Clark's eyes met mine, a sharp pain shot up my back. It was as if someone was sticking me with a needle.

"Come girl...don't be shy, come closer"

The pain grew in intensity as I inched closer to the bed. As I made my approach, the cleanliness of the room stood out to me. Everything was in its designated place, and the bed's sheets were snugly tucked under the bed frame. It was as if no one truly lived in the room.

As if it was just for show.

Once I was within arm's reach, Mrs. Clark's hand gently stroked against the side of my dress. Her fingers had a slight pressure that forced stillness upon me. Refusing the instinct to shiver, I raised my head and held her gaze.

"Lift up your dress," she ordered after a brief moment of silence.

"Excuse me ma'a-"

"I *said* lift up your dress and turn to face away from me...now."

She did not raise her voice, but a part of me wished she had. The calm tone felt out of place and caused my hands to reach for something that was, at the moment, pooled on the floor. Now completely bare, with my back turned towards her, I closed my eyes and began to count. I could feel her eyes on me, but all else was quiet. The light brush of her breath on my shoulder was the only indication that she had moved from the bed. After what felt like an eternity, Mrs. Clark finally revealed her intentions.

"You did well today. Actually followed orders...unlike most of the animals around here."

I flinched.

However," there was a faint jangle of something being pulled from a drawer, "there is one last thing I must teach you, a lesson that all new house slaves learn."

WHAP

That was the only warning I got before the sting of leather connecting with my flesh overtook my senses.

WHAP

Small, thin strips

WHAP

Knotted strips

WHAP

Thick strips

WHAP

A singular, thick braid

WHAP

Large and flat

WHAP

The hits seemed never ending as she taught me the differences between her *"toys"*. Tears streamed down my face. I counted each one as it crashed to the floor.

Chapter 9

Betsie

"I'm worried 'bout Eva."

"I know ma, me too. I think this place is finally starting to get to her," my son whispered as he paced around the kitchen house.

Dull thuds pierced the resulting silence as I sliced through yam after yam. Although my hands were busy, my eyes stayed glued to Jacob. He stomped so hard that dust rose with each step.

"Boy will ya please stop pacin'! That's not helpin' nobody. All it's doin' is makin' me nervous!"

I placed the yam pieces in a little bowl full of water beside me. Reaching for another, I turned my attention back to making dinner.

"...and of course dis place is gettin' to her. She's been thrust inta an unknown environment, been beaten, is frightened most likely, and on top of that, she's gone to 40 burials in tha span of 4 months. Seein' that much death..."

My hands shook as the words left my mouth, forcing me to place the knife on the counter and take a deep breath.

"Seein' slave after slave leave dis place...it can't be good fo' her health. Heck, it ain't good fo' anybody's health. But not everyone copes tha same...not everyone can handle it."

"I think she can handle it ma. She's strong - I sensed it the night we met...."

Confidence radiated out of his tone, but the look on his face begged to differ. Jacob had finally stopped burning a hole in the floor. He was now sitting on a bench in the corner, his knee tapping like a woodpecker.

"...but," he continued on, "she hasn't been to our dinners in a while and

I'd feel better if I just saw her with my own eyes."

"I don't doubt her strength, son. She may just need sum time to herself fo' she comes back 'round. Besides," I jokingly added, "she won't be able to keep up or improve her strength if she doesn't start eating soon."

"She's not eating?" Jacob's foot stilled.

Something in the way he responded forced me to give him my full attention. Setting down my makeshift knife once more, my eyes held Jacob's. They had darkened to an almost imperceptible black, pupil and iris becoming one as they normally did when he was serious. I had half a mind to reveal I had only been teasing him, and that Eva was in fact eating. However, the glassy glint that passed over Jacob's eyes had me holding my tongue.

My son had an idea...and I intended on seeing how it would all pan out.

Chapter 10

Eva

Ever since that first day of work, I felt myself shutting down. Jacob and Ms. Betsie had been a silent well of support. They didn't push me to talk. They waited for me to sort through the complexity of my thoughts and feelings, but by their glances, I could tell I was starting to worry them. The look of pity that had taken over Jacob's face when he saw my scars that second night had compelled me to avoid him over the last few months. For some reason, I wanted him to see strength when he looked at me, not damage.

My mind constantly raced. It's inability to be still kept me up at night.

I tried to sort through the craziness in my head as I washed dishes in the main house. The simplicity of dragging a cloth back and forth over the porcelain gave me something simple to focus on. Standing in front of one of the large bay windows on the first floor, I had a great view of the crop fields - the sun warmed my skin and the sugar cane swayed slightly in the wind. It would have been a welcomed sight had I not watched a man and woman be dragged lifeless from those fields not more than 3 days ago. Glancing back down at the plate in my hands, I moved to dry it when a soft tap on the window drew my attention. Looking up, I almost dropped the dish when Jacob's face filled my vision. My first instinct was to ignore him and continue my task.

I'm in the middle of work - I don't want to get into any trouble.

But my mother hadn't raised me to be rude. So, after a quick glance behind me, I lifted the latch and pushed the window open. Jacob stepped closer as I inched back, my eyes refusing to look at him. I waited for him to speak, to reveal why he was standing in front of this window instead of tending to the horses. Instead, only silence ensued. Curiosity won over embarrassment as my head slowly lifted to meet Jacob's face. The smirk that I found almost made me forget everything

...almost.

Fighting off the urge to smile, I turned to anger. Steeling my face, I placed the now dry plate on top of the others and opened my mouth.

"What are you doing here Jacob, don't you have somewhere to be? If the masters of the house, or worse Damien, finds you out here talking to me, we are both going to be skinned alive!"

Cold fury seeped from my words as I ripped my gaze from his chin. My hand reached for another dirty plate and dunked it into the water basin. My hands had barely grazed the soapy water when Jacob's soft, but commanding voice reached out.

"Eva," he whispered, luring my attention back to him.

He had moved to stand up against the window, his elbows resting atop the window seal. My eyes only narrowed at him in response. I envied how calm, confident, and in control he seemed despite his situation. He was at ease and I was on edge. He smirked as I finally raised my eyes to be level with his.

That's when the smell hit me.

My mouth watered and from the corner of my eye, I caught a glimpse of what seemed to be a small wrapped package in Jacob's hand.

"What is that?"

"Oh this?"

Being eye to eye, I could see the depths of his irises darken into a starless night as he answered, "this is something I made for you. Ma told me you weren't eating, and I hadn't seen you in a while, so I thought to bring you this. Wanted to make sure you ate. I remembered you telling ma about your favorite dish from home, something called ‘congri’ I believe. Rice and beans you said, so I attempted to make the Jamaican version of it...I thought it would remind you of home.”

Words spilled from Jacob’s mouth like a waterfall. If I hadn’t known any better, I could have sworn a light blush spread across his cheeks. Blaming the sun and heat, I shook the thought from my head and tried to focus on what he was now saying.

“And while having you worry about my well-being is great, you don’t have to stress about my duties. I told the Masta I was sick and that was all he needed to hear to urge me to stay away from his horses for the day.”

Apparently done explaining himself, Jacob reached in past the window and placed the parcel on the counter next to me.

I had no idea what he was talking about when he mentioned me not eating, but telling him he was wrong about that was the farthest thing from my mind. Blinking back the stinging feeling coming from my eyes, I snatched up the parcel and held it softly to my chest with one hand.

"You did this to remind me of where I come from?" My voice strained to come out.

"Of course, I wanted… after everything, I wanted to do something nice."

With that, I couldn't help the single tear that fell from my eye and the smile that finally returned to my face. Seeing a glimpse of my old self, Jacob gave me a full-toothed grin. His eyes sparkled as stars returned to his night sky. I jumped when Jacob's calloused hand settled over mine. The warmth of his palm urged me to return the touch, clasping my hand tight to his. We stood there, just smiling at each other and holding hands. The light that had evaded me for the past four and a half months was finally returning. And for the very first time, I allowed myself to get caught up in that feeling.

How could I have known we weren’t truly alone.

Chapter 11

Someone Is Always Watching

SNAP

A twig broke under my weight as I shifted into a better position. Jacob and that new slave...

Hmm, what is her name? Eva, maybe?

...they both turned towards my general direction, but I knew they couldn't see me. They were too engrossed in conversation to even truly notice they were being watched. And after all these years, no one had ever caught me. Despite that certainty, I inched deeper into the hedges that provided my cover. From my vantage point, I could see everything. Jacob handed the new one a package - they were now holding hands and laughing. Mister Clark would want news of this immediately. He would not enjoy the way in which Jacob smiled at her - not at all.

I'll have to keep an eye on them both.

Chapter 12

Eva

Currently, Mrs. Clark sat in a chair in front of me, dressed only in her nightgown. Her straw-colored hair fell loosely across her shoulders. The outfit that I would soon help Mrs. Clark into sat cleanly across the bed behind me. My fingers still ached from each wrinkle I personally pressed out earlier that morning. As I combed through Mrs. Clark's locks, I was shocked by the tenderness that I showed her. I'd only been here for a little over seven months now and even with all the cruelty she had shown me, I felt a connection to her. I knew almost everything about her, how she liked three sugar cubes in her coffee, hated eggs, enjoyed warm baths in the evenings, read before bed, and desired chicken for almost every meal.

One stroke.

Two strokes.

Three strokes.

Four.

My fingers gently worked through any serious tangles before following up with the brush. All was quiet except for the soft crunch of my movements. Each pass through her hair was a lull to sleep. On the rare occasion I dared risk eye contact, I often found Mrs. Clark drifting off. Today was no different. I watched through the mirror as Mrs. Clark's eyes closed. Her shoulders slumped and her breathing evened out. This was normally the time when she opened herself up to me and my touch. Her morning dress routine was a brief moment where she was vulnerable and at my mercy.

I often asked myself, how could she trust me - someone she hated. She hated me and I…

I hated, yet cared for her.

It makes no sense.

Chapter 13

Eva

After dressing and pampering Mrs. Clark, I visited Betsie in the kitchen. I figured I could aid her in preparing the Clarks' lunches. Betsie stood in front of the counter, her back turned to me. The melodic hum that escaped her lips was unfamiliar, but soothing as I strode into the room. I quickly kissed Betsie on the cheek as I stepped around her to place Mrs. Clark's breakfast tray into the sink.

"And what was that fo'," Betsie asked, her hands working dough as she smiled in my direction.

"Oh that," I started, grinning down into the shine of the sink, "that was for just being you Ms. Betise."

Silence ensued as Betsie and I shared a brief look. Neither one of us said anything, but from the glint in her eyes, I knew she understood.

I lo- .... cared about her.

Just thinking the words had me rubbing my palms over my trousers and had my heart fluttering to the point I thought I might faint. Betsie didn't seem to notice the hand I sat upon the counter to support me. Her attention had returned to kneading the dough in front of her. It's not something I could ever admit outloud, the fear of forming new connections held my tongue, but despite my hesitations and walls, Betsie and her son had wiggled through the cracks. It had been two weeks since Jacob's kindness, but the weight of his actions had still not left me - they fueled me through many tough days and nights on the plantation. Thinking of those who were in my corner gave me strength: those like Betsie, Jacob, and most recently Mary (although hers was a quiet solace). They had become an integral part of my existence on the Clark plantation.

Reasons for me to keep going.

After taking a moment to steady myself, I flew into the lulling motions of washing the dishes. I had just sat a dried teacup back into the cupboard when Betsie addressed me.

"So Ms. Eva, what are you thinkin' we should make Mistress Clark for lunch? I already sent a sandwich up fo' Masta."

I turned from the cupboards to find Betsie already looking at me.

"Chicken," we uttered in unison, bursting out in quiet laughter.

"Well since that's settled, I'll get started on tha chicken and carrots, but after ya' finish washin' those dishes could ya' rinse the beans and thro 'em in a pot fo' me?"

"Sure thing Ms. Betsie!"

Turning back to our respective tasks, I listened to the sweet song Ms. Betsie hummed while we worked. It was a soft tune, lest Mr. and Mrs. Clark hear, but each note came out perfect and pure.

Next time we have dinner I'm gonna ask her to teach it to me.

My hands shook with the weight of the food on the silver tray I eased up the steps with.

Ms. Betsie outdid herself today!

The china lightly rattled as it rocked against the silver. Reaching the top of the steps, I took a deep breath, focussing on the slight rise and fall of my chest. With my hands still and my footsteps light, I headed towards Mistress Clark's room. My hand was poised to knock, when a giant crash rang out. I could hear the pieces of whatever broke skitter across the floor.

"Shut up, you aren't smart or skilled enough to be talking to me about this," Mr. Clark screamed.

SLAP

My hand lowered. Silence ensued as I pressed my ear to the door.

"Don't forget that I owned my father's plantation and had my own tavern before I married you Jim Clark." I could hear the hurt in the Mistress' voice, but her words came out hard and sharp like steel. "I have money of my own and know more than you think. Ha, I even know about your problems with Hercules...you remember that next time, before you question my intelligence."

Hercules?

I hadn't heard that name before, but the fact that he seemed to be causing problems for Mr. Clark had me hanging onto it like a lifeline. I pressed closer to try and hear more, but the sound of heavy boots walking towards the door forced me to jump back, almost dropping the tray of food. The door, thankfully, did not open. However, the damage was done - I had been frightened to death. Placing the food in front of the door, I clutched my chest. My heart banged an erratic rhythm under my hand - this time, the fear of getting caught outweighed my curiosity. I had succeeded in avoiding Mr. Clark as much as possible over the course of the past couple of months. The most time I spent with him since arriving on the plantation was during dinner in which I occasionally had to serve him. However, on those nights, I made sure to make myself scarce as soon as my serving duties were over. While a big part of me begged to stay and hear out the end of their conversation, I had no intention of being face to face with Mr. Clark anytime soon. Thus, I knocked twice and briskly retreated back to the main floor.

Chapter 14

Eva

The rest of my day was blissfully uneventful. After overhearing the strange altercation between Mr. and Mrs. Clark, I made sure to busy myself with laundry, dishes, dusting, and taking inventory of all our produce. I even had time to help Mary out in the Mistress' garden - a welcomed break from being cooped up in the house. Mary and I tended to several plants, from sweet potatoes, to yams, maize, guava, passion fruit, and even peppers. Having dirt between my fingers again was cathartic and was the only time I'd allow myself to think of the family I had lost. I no longer felt a sharp pain in my heart when I thought of them. I was making progress towards moving on with my life; thus, there was now just a dull throb where their love should have been.

Mrs. Clark didn't call on me very much for the rest of the day. Only once was my presence requested and it was to deliver a handful of ice wrapped in some cloth. With very few distractions, I breezed through my daily duties. The bottom end of the sun was just grazing the horizon by the time my work was done. Wanting to escape the house, I made my way down the grand staircase to await Betsie. Reaching the bottom, I leaned against a stone post to my right. Although hard, the structure eased the stiffness working its way into my shoulders. Wiping my hands along my beige trousers, I took a moment to breathe fully. I allowed myself to sag against the structure, eyes closing as I basked in the fleeting sunlight.

That's when the hairs on my arms stood straight up.

A feeling akin to being dunked in cold water eased down my spine, and I twirled around to face the intruder.

Two icy blue eyes held mine.

My heart dropped seeing *him* standing but two feet away from me. His face held no emotion, but his eyes raged like a lethal blizzard. My hand stretched for the hem of my blouse and my leg began to twitch. I was glued to my spot, helpless, as Mr. Clark stalked towards me.

"Eva," he began.

Resisting the urge to flinch, I dared hold his gaze, "Master."

The smell of rum hit me first as he closed the distance between us. I had only ever tasted the drink once, back in Cuba, and I had never drank enough to ever smell like Mr. Clark. His moves were slow, a bit shaky but calculating, as his gaze slid up and down my frame.

"You need to come with me, now," he growled. His voice had an edge to it that I had never heard before.

Not even when he was arguing with his wife earlier.

It was this tone that forced my legs to obey.

"Where are y-y-you taking me," I whispered as I passed him. I shuddered at the whimper that escaped my lips, frustrated at the weakness I laid bare.

"Walk." His arm pointed up towards the mill and kogehus.

He said nothing else and the rest of the journey was made in silence. When Mr. Clark pushed open the door to the kogehus, a sweltering heat attacked me. My skin became slick with moisture, my clothes clung to my skin in a sticky mess, and beads of sweat dripped from my brow.

This is unbearable.

My eyes flickered to the brown bodies that littered the space in front of me. Many were shirtless, men and women, and despite the heat they worked at a pace that should have been impossible.

They have to, or they die - my mind reasoned.

A hard push from behind ripped me from my thoughts as I faltered. That shove was just what I needed for my own preservation instincts to kick in.

"You know M-m-master, I really should be getting back to t-t-the Mistress. She had some work for me to do when t-t-the sun went down and I-I-I should get on that or she'll be right mad with m-m-me."

I turned to face Mr. Clark. My head had barely rotated when out the corner of my eye, I saw his hand reach out. I was too slow to react. He snagged my blouse, pulled, and twisted. In one heartbeat I had been in front of him, in the next we had swapped places and I was now behind. The force of the move caused my feet to tangle over themselves and I crashed to the floor. My shoulder screamed as I landed with a hard thud. Mr. Clark's hands on me never loosened. With a steel grip, he dragged my body across the floor, avoiding machinery and vat after vat of molten sugar juice as he led me deeper into the kogehus. My legs and arms flailed, I reached out to find purchase on something, anything. My heart beat so loudly, I had no clue whether or not I was screaming. Unfortunately, my eyes still worked just fine.

They darted back and forth, pleading with the individuals that worked the kogehus. Panic threatened to take over as each and every person ignored my cries. Bodies flinched and some may have moved towards my direction, but upon seeing Mr. Clark, they all turned their backs on me.

Coldness in such a hot place.

Tears or sweat stung my eyes and my last thought before being pulled into a room was:

There are scars and burns on every back turned.

Chapter 15

Eva

No windows, two doors.

I knelt in a dark room at the back of the kogehus, the only light came from a raging fire pit directly in front of me. Dirt was caked on my skin and clothes, my sweat acting as a glue. My trousers had survived, but I could feel the slightest chill from a rip on the back of my blouse - *where his hands had been.*

Mr. Clark had thrown me in the middle of the room, retreating to a space in between the firepit and the door we had just entered. The shadows cast from the fire danced across his face, flickering him in and out of focus. My eyes drifted over to the second door across from the first. There was no time to even consider escape as the door flung open, orange light flooding the tiny room. A monster of a man stood just outside the door frame, his head cut off by the top of it. Bending over, he entered the room. His presence filled the space…and not in the light and airy way in which Betsie's did. His presence suffocated and extinguished. My eyes fluttered as I adjusted to the sudden intrusion of light and my shoulders heaved as the man Betsie had warned me to stay away from all those months ago now loomed in front of me.

Damien

The man's skin mirrored the sun. It wasn't a golden tan like the Clarks, but more red and blotchy. A thin sheen of sweat coated his skin. A gloved hand came up to brush over his short, dark brown hair. His green eyes were pointed in my direction. The sharp stare he gave me had just as much bite to it as Mr. Clark's. My chest expanded, but refused to collapse back under the weight of both men's scrutiny. Pain danced along the edge of my subconsciousness. Looking down, I saw little droplets of red littering the edge of my shirt. The pads of my thumb and forefinger were raw and pink. The silence was deafening. Not one word was spoken between the two men, but all it took was a slight nod from Mr. Clark for Damien to move. His steps were slow and domineering as he made his way over to the firepit. Reaching behind it, into an unknown space, he pulled out what looked to be a long metal stick. Thrusting the other end into the pit, he glanced in my direction. Orange and red reflected back at me. Little beads of sweat reformed along the bottom of my lip and at the base of my neck. Despite the heat, a chill rushed down my spine. Mr. Clark's study of me had not wavered.

In the blink of an eye, he rushed me. The action was so quick, I barely moved two inches before he was on me. Mr. Clark's sweaty hands clasped onto both of my arms, trapping them to my chest. Pressing a knee onto my back, he ensured my immobility. A sound of desperation escaped my lips. My eyes locked on the door until a hefty force knocked my head back so hard, I threatened to black out. My body denied me that grace as my head lolled to one side.

Still conscious.

Damien now loomed in front of me. Only the right side of his body was visible to me with my right eye now throbbing and heavy, its vision dark. Blood dribbled from the corner of my mouth, a red stream pooling on the stone floor. Mr. Clark's hands were still firmly holding me in place, his surprisingly sharp nails bit into me. A second pair of hands brushed across my back. Every muscle in my body solidified as those hands tore my shirt to pieces, leaving me bare. Instinctively, I struggled to cover myself, but Mr. Clark's hold only tightened. Damien positioned himself behind me. Seeing was getting harder and harder, but I could feel Mr. Clark's eyes locked on to my chest. A third hand, Damien's hand, reached around to cover my mouth when a searing pain ripped through my right shoulder. The smell of burning flesh assaulted my senses and brought bile to the back of my throat. My muffled screams were all I remembered before my mind fell into darkness.

Chapter 16

Eva

Pain is all I should have felt, but hatred fed the fire that now burned inside me. Cradling my right side, I limped further into the murk of the night. Both arms were wrapped tight across the front of my chest. My right eye was swollen shut. It was difficult to judge where exactly I was going, but thankfully my legs moved of their own volition. They led me back to my quarters. My mind however was empty. Not a calming emptiness like when at peace, but something hollow and cavernous.

It was as if my mind ripped out pieces of itself, parts of my emotions, to keep me functioning. The soft rustle of the sugar cane stalks was the only thing that registered in my mind, the only thing that told me this was real.

Before I knew it, my legs brought me to a door, a door that could have been mine if not for the sun etched deeply into the wood above my head. A heat took over my body at the sight of it and with the last ounces of my strength, I pushed. The door swung open so hard, it rattled on its hinges. Four eyes whipped to my position in the door frame. A small cry escaped Ms. Betsie's lips as she took me in, but none of us dared move. Shock no doubt held them in their place, but anger kept me in mine.

"W-w-why?"

Black spots danced along the edge of my vision.

"Why didn't you tell me this is what he does?" I spat.

That was all I was able to get out before fatigue overtook me. My knees buckled and the ground swept out from beneath me. I landed up against something hard, yet warm, and then my head rolled back into darkness.

Chapter 17

Eva

Nothing.

That's what went through my head when I passed out, not a single thing.

My eyes fluttered open to a soft, cool pressure on my forehead. Only a sliver of candlelight reached me through the mess that was now my right eye. Blinking slowly, my left eye finally focused on the form in front of me. Ms. Betsie sat on a stool beside me. Her head hung low, her hands were wrung together, and little creases littered her forehead. Looking down at myself, I saw that my tattered blouse and trousers had been replaced.

Betsie must have washed and dressed me.

That's when I noticed the dull, stinging ache emanating from my right shoulder. My voice caught as I breathed through the pain and started to reach for the area. The sudden, albeit slow, movement must have alerted Betsie because with an inhuman speed, her hand darted out to stop mine.

"Child, no."

Her tone, like her grip on my wrist, was soft. But because anger still burned through me, lurking beneath my skin, I twisted out of her grasp and defiantly reached for my shoulder.

I regretted it immediately.

Brushing up against the area, a searing pain shot through me. My right hand clenched into a fist on instinct. My fingers crossed over my scabbed, tender skin. It felt cracked, raw, and there was something sticky all along the area. Despite the mess of flesh, the letters there on my shoulder were unmistakable.

JC

Jim Clark

Tears begged to fall, but my anger at everyone and everything burned them away, denying me relief. Seeing the wetness trapped within my eye, Betsie soon reached over to pull my hand away from the mark.

"That's enough, Eva."

I ripped my hand out of hers, but cooperated, letting my arm fall back to my side. Satisfied, Betsie reached down beside her to grab a small container. Scooping a coin sized amount onto her fingertips, she rolled me onto my left side. I jumped at the expected pain, but relief and a surprising coolness was all that came.

"Sinkle," Betsie declared.

Aloe

I couldn't see Betsie, but could feel the soft, yet purposeful motions of her hands as she coated my brand. Filing the silence, she continued on:

"I'm puttin' sum more sinkle salve on tha wound. It should aid tha healin' process and should ease sum of yo' pain, but you need not touch it and it'll be sore to tha touch for awhile."

Content in her work, she guided me onto my back and eased into the stool beside where I lay. Looking at her, I could see the sadness in her eyes. It consumed the normal light found in her brown depths.

"I'm so sorry."

The whisper that escaped her lips was so quiet that had we been anywhere else, it could have been the wind. However, as the words registered, my hands flexed back into fists. Holding my breath, I tried to still the emotions swirling inside me.

Pain.

Sadness.

Fury.

Betsie pleaded with her eyes for me to say anything, but wanting Betsie to speak her piece, I kept my lips sealed.

"I am so so sorry child. When ya weren't outside tha main house on tha steps like you said after our duties, I thought….I thought ya had just left without me. Th-That ya grew tired of waitin' fo' me, and I thought nothin' more of it."

Her gaze was genuine, mine hardened.

That's why she thinks I'm angry?

A laugh threatened to escape my lips.

That is the farthest thing from my mind. Ha…I had actually forgotten that I was waiting for her when this whole thing started.

As I focussed back on Betsie, her eyes were red and little droplets of water streamed down her face. I blinked several times, trying to validate the strange sight. Tears in Betsie's eyes?

It looked unnatural.

My heart leapt at the sight and the urge to reach out and place my hand over hers rose. Despite the inner softening, my gaze stayed hard and my fists clenched. There was still a fire within me and it refused to dissipate so quickly. With its encouraging warmth, a new dam fortified around my heart.

This one will be stronger.

For a tense minute, our eyes warred before she continued on. Her's pleaded, mine's denied.

"If I had known Eva, I would have-"

"You would have what!?" I spat, my blood boiling.

The bite in my voice caused Betsie to jump. Her mouth opened as if she was going to respond, but just as quickly, it snapped shut. She grew very quiet then and her head fell to look away from me.

The woman of a thousand words had none for me in that moment.

Betise's silence spoke volumes and when she finally did meet my piercing gaze, we both knew the answer.

"I know you're mad at me," she whispered as her lower lip quivered, "but I truly am sorry."

With her words she reached out, hesitant for the first time, and placed her hand over mine. I didn't flinch, didn't jerk back, didn't respond at all. Instead, I turned my head away and focussed my hazy gaze on the opposite wall of Betsie's hut. My shoulder protested at the movement, but I refused to show any discomfort. In spite of my coldness, regardless of the hardness I wanted to convey, a tiny crack spidered along my inner walls. Removing her hand, Betsie reached for the cloth on my forehead. Although I refused to look her head on, I could see her from the corner of my eye. She stood with the cloth in hand and walked over to a bucket near the door. She dunked the cloth in a few times, wrung it out, and then returned to my side, gently placing the cloth back on my head. This time, she made sure it covered my right eye. The wet cloth soothed my skin and, regrettably, my emotions. With my right eye covered, my left began to hone in on its surroundings and that's when I noticed it. In the leftmost corner of the room, by the door, pieces of wood littered the ground. I could only make out the splintered legs of what most likely used to be a stool.

"That's Jacob's doing," Betsie responded as she noticed my lingering gaze on the scene.

Just noticing the man's absence, my eyes snapped back to Betsie and my heart began to beat faster.

"Where is he now?"

"I sent him away, back to his hut."

Panic bubbled through me and I couldn't stop the outburst that came next:

"You left him alone!"

The indignation in my voice caused Betsie to falter, her next words interrupted. Her mouth closed as she studied me intently. After an uncomfortable moment, a small smile graced her face. It was so brief, I would have missed it had I not been looking at her. My outburst not only gave Betsie pause, it scared me too.

Why that reaction, at a time like this...

That's as far as my mind got before a sharp pain ripped my focus away. Breathing deep, I tried to focus on Betsie's next words.

"Don't worry child, George is watchin' over Jacob. Other than catchin' you when ya collapsed at tha door and placin' you here on dis bed, he was no help at all. I had to send him away. But I couldn't have him gettin' worked up and doin' somthin' stupid, so...I sent George to go watch him," Betsie's eyes closed as she shook her head. When she opened them to look at me, the smirk from earlier had returned, "I fear in tha name of your honor Eva, my son would do many stupid things."

At her words, my body went numb. I could feel the crack in my walls widen.

My left hand found its way to the hem of my shirt as I whispered, "Why would he get that upset over me?"

"Ha, that boy is infatuated wit ya, you are his center Eva. He just doesn't want to admit it because…" the light in Betsie's eyes dimed and her smile faltered, "because findin' love in a place like dis is like findin' water in tha hottest of desserts. It's precious and exhilarating, it gives people hope. Unfortunately, dis place is not tha best nurturer of hope. He's afraid of losing ya, and so the stubborn boy has convinced himself it's betta off not givin' in to his emotions....Maybe ya can show him otherwise?"

Betsie's gaze held mine and the weight of the moment pressed hard on my chest.

Crack

"Because life here on dis plantation, Eva, is too short."

For the first time, a comfortable silence fell between us. I was at a loss for words and had no idea how to respond. So focusing in on my breathing, I watched as Betsie tidied up her hut. It wasn't until Betsie returned with a freshly dipped cloth that the question I had been dying to ask finally reached my lips. The words softly spilled out.

"Why didn't you warn me?"

After placing the cloth atop my head, she sat back in her stool and her hands fell to her sides. Sorrow plagued her face as I said, “I thought we were friends, I thought we were family?”

Crack

The water behind the dam within me broke free and everything I had been holding in came rushing out. My tears were finally released and fell in silent streams. The anger in me was doused out, leaving only hurt and betrayal. A sob threatened to rack through me when Betsie’s strong arms wrapped around me.

“Oh child no, that’s what ya thought we did? No, I swear we had no idea Master Clark was goin’ to do that to ya! I’ve only seen those who have committed a serious offense, like run away, be branded. I had no reason to think to warn ya because you have done nothin’ wrong. There was no reason fo’ dis. Even wit all tha trouble my son gets inta, he has neva been branded. Neither have I. The fact that Master Clark did -”

Betsie paused, her eyebrows knitting in thought.

"Wh-what are you thinking Ms. Betsie, what does it mean," I sniffed.

"It means," she refused to meet my gaze, "nothin' ya don't already know." Looking me right in the eye, she continued on, "I don't know if it's possible, but I would suggest ya try and stay as far away from Mr. Clark as possible."

Chapter 18

Eva

I decided the best way to take Betsie's advice was to throw myself into work, keep as busy as possible, and stay far away from dinner service. A week after the incident, Betsie and I convinced Mrs. Clark to move me onto kitchen clean-up duty during dinner. That conversation was a weird one. I had asked Betsie to come with me because she had known Mrs. Clark longer than I and could help sell her on the change in tasks. Surprisingly though, Betsie's aid wasn't needed. Ever since the branding, Mrs. Clark had been extremely generous in the altering of my schedule. I'd dare say she has even been kinder when interacting with me. The night after my experience with Damien and Mr. Clark, I was finishing up some dusting in the foyer when the strangest thing happened. Bruises littered my body and their aches slowed my movements. Because of that, I was still working through my chores even though the sun had long set. I had only been dusting for a short while before Mrs. Clark called upon me. Finding me in the foyer, she wordlessly got my attention, motioned for me to follow, and then turned on her heel. Although my feet immediately started after her, my mind pleaded the opposite. Beads of sweat formed at the base of my neck and my heartbeat quicked. I thought I was going to faint, remembering the night before - what had happened when a Clark asked me to follow them.

Despite my nervousness, I tried to steady my breathing by counting my steps as Mrs. Clark led me down the hallway. Opening the door to the basement, she gestured for me to go first then closed and locked the door behind us. When the lock clicked into place, I flinched and my hand flew to the edge of my blouse. When I made it down the two flights of steps, a large bin of clothes and a wooden rocking chair sat in the center of the room.

Laundry? She wants me to do laundry at this hour?

“Mistress, I-I-I apologize. I-I-I didn’t know there w-w-was more laundry to be done. Earlier, I only w-w-washed the clothes you left in t-t-the bin outside of your suite as always. I h-h-had no ide-”

Mrs. Clark’s raised hand silenced me.

“These are some last minute additions,” she responded, “don’t fret over what you did before, just work on these now.”

Mrs. Clark didn’t move to strike me, nor did she say anything further. She just gestured to the washing bin closest to the rocking chair. Relieved that I wasn’t going to be beaten or punished, I gently slid the clothes towards the washing bin and gratefully took my place in front of it.

Laundry I can do.

I expected Mrs. Clark to leave me to my task; thus, I was shocked when she instead sat in the rocking chair beside me. She had produced a book from somewhere and was now intently reading it. I had gotten about a fourth of the way through the stack of clothes when the soap bar I was using had run out. Using the wash bin for support, I reached for the extra bars of soap along the wall. My knees protested with the effort. They were so sore that I had just grazed a bar of soap when my left knee gave out and I slipped on a small puddle of water. Thankfully, I was able to get my arms out in front of me and brace myself. However, the force of the fall caused my blouse to shift, exposing my shoulders. Feeling the cool air hit my brand, I rushed to cover it up. But before I could lift the top end of my blouse, a dainty hand wrapped around my wrist.

She's touching me - Mrs. Clark is touching me.

There was no force behind her grip, just enough pressure to still me. My eyes locked in on her hand, her light-golden skin in stark contrast with the almond tone of mine. I dared not move, nor breathe. I was curious as to what she would do next. Assured that I would not move, Mrs. Clark released me from her hold and ghosted her fingers over my mark. With my shoulder still tender, I flinched at the light contact. Every muscle in my body tensed. This was the first time she had ever made any contact with me in all seven months of me working for her. I was equally shocked and moved by the tenderness in her touch. That was when she spoke.

"This, this is why you are here," she whispered as she stroked over the two letters once more.

Her words confused me and were enough to bring me out of my haze.

My brand is the reason why I am in the basement doing laundry?

I angled my head in Mrs. Clark's direction, anxious to ask the questions speeding through my mind. She must have sensed my curiosity because before I could even open my mouth, she removed her hand from my shoulder and composed herself.

"Get. Back. To work."

Mrs. Clark didn't yell, but there was enough force in her voice that I knew not to say anything more. And just like that, whatever had occurred between us was over. She sat back in her rocking chair and focused on her book. I quickly fixed my blouse, grabbed the new soap bar that had skidded to the floor, and went on washing the clothes before me. Mrs. Clark didn't speak to or acknowledge me for the rest of the night. We passed the time it took me to complete my task in a strangely comfortable silence. After I had finally been released for the day and was making my way back to my quarters, I couldn't help but feel like I had just seen a different side to my cruel mistress.

From that point on, Mrs. Clark called on me to wash every night. At sundown, right after dinner, I would head to the basement and work through clothes for what felt like at least two hours. Mrs. Clark stayed down there with me each and every time. We never talked, she would just sit and read or knit. Sometimes she would even slip into slumber and I would often lose myself in the mundane task. It was somewhat peaceful.

Mrs. Clark and I's relationship wasn't the only one altered by my branding. Betsie did all that she could to keep me out of sight whenever Mr. Clark was around. Even Mary did her part to help me avoid him. News must have traveled fast between slaves because when I had reached my cabin after washing clothes with Mrs. Clark that first night, I found Mary waiting at my door for me. It was so out of character that I immediately thought something was wrong, or someone had died. But as soon as I rushed to her, she handed me a small copper tin and a parcel. I later found out that the copper tin was full of Sinkle, Aloe, and she had given me 2 strips of salted mackerel and a couple of sweet potatoes from her bi-monthly food rations. Mary didn't say anything either, just held eye contact with me and clasped her hands over mine. Her gifts were cradled between our joined hands. We stood like that for at least a minute and then Mary silently let go and slipped into the night. From that point on, in addition to my new washing schedule, Mary decided to come up with an alarm system for me. Despite her timidness, she used her daily task of tending to the garden as a way to scope out when Mr. Clark was on his way back to the house. If she spotted him, she'd imitate the calls of the purple/blue headed hummingbirds we'd often see around the plantation. I was grateful for her support and in turn tried my best to be there for her whenever she needed.

Unfortunately, my branding affected Jacob the hardest. He started to accompany me home every night, no matter how late. He didn't walk right beside me for fear that someone would see us together, but he was always watching. Either from within the cover of the sugar cane stalks, or feet away as he pretended to walk the horses, he was always there in case I needed assistance. It was a comfort to know he had my back, but a voice deep within knew better than to relax even with Jacob's watchful eye. Because if I was taken once again, I knew that Jacob wouldn't be able to stop the act from happening. I would never really be safe if Damien or Mr. Clark came for me.

The distant and empty eyes of those slaves who watched me be dragged, kicking and screaming, to the back of the kogehus came to mind at that moment.

If it happened again, no one could save me.

Despite my fears, and with the help of my second kin, days soon turned into weeks and weeks to months without ever laying eyes on Mr. Clark. It had been two months since the incident and while I believed in my evasion abilities, I was still shocked that he had let me be. I told myself he was just busy dealing with the recent incidents on the plantation. For example, two days ago, I was tasked with delivering some items from the market to Mrs. Clark. When I knocked on her door, I found her room to be empty. I quickly entered, left her items on the side table where she could see them, and left. As I turned to head back towards the steps, candlelight at the end of the hall drew my attention. I couldn't help but inch closer and at the farthest end of the second-floor hall, I found the door to Mr. Clark's study open. That door had been mysteriously locked since the day I arrived. I quickly looked behind me for Mr. and Mrs. Clark. Listening out for the slightest of movements and hearing none, my curiosity won out over reason. Taking a deep breath I eased the door open. The room was huge. There was a small bookshelf in the right back corner and a fireplace off to the left. It was framed by a long couch and two smaller ones. Near the fireplace was another door, this one closed. I had no idea where it led to. In front of the longest couch was a small table. A glass filled with what looked to be rum rested on top of it. A huge oak desk took up the center of the room, a candle within a silver holder sat burning towards the edge. Several small items littered Mr. Clark's desk, but what stood out to me was a white feather sitting in a flat, ornate metal piece. It lured me further into the room and I swept my hands across the contraption. A beautiful design I had never seen before was etched into the metal surface. A small smile came to my lips as I took in the rest of this space and that's when I saw it. My eyes caught on a small slip of paper at the corner of the desk. It was angled as if someone had tossed it aside in disgust. I still failed to hear footsteps, so, carefully as to not touch the note, I leaned over the edge of the desk and read.

We lost five barrels of grain and countless supplies are missing. The southernmost patch of sugarcane is burnt to a crisp - I am still sifting through the ash for casualties. Isiah, Pete, and I are searching the woods for the culprits. We'll be sending out a hunting party at the end of the week.

- Damien

My mind was reeling.

Missing supplies? Burnt fields? Hunting for something? Could this have to do with that Hercules Mrs. Clark mentioned months ago?

I scanned my eyes across the note again, wanting to parse out the few words I hadn't understood. It was then however, that I heard a creaking noise coming from the closed door at my back. My heart plummeted, but I did not hesitate. As light and as fast as I could, I flew through the open door, crept across the hallway, and sped down the steps. I didn't release my breath until my feet were safely back on the main floor.

Chapter 19

Eva

My weekly dinners with Betsie and Jacob were the only things I looked forward to. Tonight, I sat next to Jacob on the dirt floor, watching as Betsie danced to beats from a makeshift drum. The fact that I hadn't gotten caught in Mr. Clark's study earlier had me vibrating with excitement. Laughter filled the air for once and I couldn't help but feel at home with these people. Although nine months ago they were only strangers, Betsie now felt like a second mother. And Jacob...well, he mattered to me as well. Knowing how important it is to find small moments of joy, we ate, joked, and danced by candlelight. I even introduced them to some of the 2-3 rhythms I had learned as a child. As the night drew on, Betsie soon retired to bed, leaving Jacob and I sitting outside of her hut. All was quiet except for the soft tune of George's successful-shift-change song in the distance. There was a slight breeze to the night air. Jacob and I sat in a pleasant silence as we took in the peaceful moment.

Well…

We sat in silence until the adrenaline from the past hour or so provided me with the courage to ask what had been on my mind for quite some time:

"What happened to your father Jacob?"

He didn't rush to answer, instead he kept his eyes focused on the stars. Their silver shine lit up his already golden skin. Jacob was silent for so long, I thought he hadn't heard me when his voice finally cut through the silence.

"My father wasn't lucky like you, mama, or me. He was a part of the gang labor system. He got really sick about a month or two before your arrival and Masta Clark moved him to the third gang,[5]"

---

[5] The **gang system** was a system of division of labor within slavery on a plantation. The third gang typically encompassed the weakest workers and were given the easiest work.

he stated. Taking a deep breath, Jacob finally turned to look at me as he continued, “His condition didn’t improve though and a week later, he was gone. Died out in the cane fields, de-weeding the crop”

Not knowing what to say, I placed a soft hand on his shoulder and held his gaze. I couldn’t tell what he was thinking, his face was devoid of all emotion. I only hoped my eyes and touch conveyed what my month refused to say. Focusing in on his eyes however, I watched as their color shifted from an aged rum to an even darker obsidian. His eyes simultaneously pierced and enveloped. Something warm, yet heavy passed between us. The weight of it snapped my hand back to my side. My cheeks quickly flushed and I nervously broke eye contact to turn my head towards the sky. Trying and failing to find relief in the cool moonlight, I attempted to change the subject.

“How did you become a carpenter Jacob? How did you prove to Mr. Clark that that was your trade?”

"Well," he responded, "Masta Clark has always been fond of me I guess, so it didn't take too much convincing on my part. I'm just good with my hands, or at least betta than most. Thankfully, I escaped the worst parts of working on a suga plantation."

I barely registered his answer as his eyes were still locked on me. I reached for the hem of my dress as I barreled into the next question.

"Well since you are such an amazing carpenter, I assume you are the one who etched that sun atop your mother's door," I inquired, gesturing behind us to the front of Betsie's door. "What's the meaning behind it?"

He must not have been expecting that question as that was what got him to finally take his eyes off of me. He glanced back at his mother's door, grinning softly. He looked completely at ease and almost boyish as I watched a memory play out across his face. It pushed a smile to my own lips and I released a breath I hadn't known I was holding as he spoke.

"You know how my mom can be a lot, how she fills up a room?" Jacob began.

He turned back towards me and his smile now lit up half of his face. I nodded quickly in agreement, eager to hear where this story was going.

"Well," he continued, "her personality reminded me of the sun. She's warm, bright, and touches a lot of people here...so I etched that sun into the top of the house when I was 8."

Laughter threatened to spill from Jacob's mouth as he recounted the tale.

"Momma was NOT pleased when I first did it. I remember her face when she came back from the Great House - Ha! I thought she was going to skin me alive...But, thankfully, she grew to love it and now every year I go and re-etch it so that it stays clearly defined."

Jacob chuckled to himself and we grinned madly at each other. I found myself laughing harder than I ever had before. My shoulders shaked and my stomach cramped as I imagined a young Jacob testing Betsie's patience. I was about to press Jacob for details about his childhood escapades when a blood-curdling scream jolted both of us into a standing position.

"What was that?" I questioned. The light and airy atmosphere from before evaporated.

"Nothing good," Jacob responded.

No sooner had the words left his mouth, than another scream rang out. This one was longer, sharper. I flinched at the sound and birds fluttered anxiously above us. A crowd of slaves had emerged from their huts. They provided a quiet buzz as we waited for a sign.

Where are the screams coming from?

Betsie stirred behind Jacob and I. Now woken from her slumber, Betsie's door creaked as she came into the moonlight. She placed a hand on my shoulder and made eye contact with her son. It seemed as if a silent conversation was being had between the two of them, and that's when the third scream reached us. It was a gut wrenching scream, and in that moment, I knew exactly where it was coming from.

The Kogehus.

It seemed as if everyone simultaneously came to the same conclusion I had; for, all the slaves who had gathered broke into a sprint. Jacob turned from his mother to quickly make eye contact with me before all three of us took off into the sugarcane. Following the crowd, we raced past stalk after stalk. The smell of manure was choking. Sugarcane leaves sliced into my face and shoulders, leaving stinging cuts in their wake. The fallen leaves and weeds tripped up many due to the moonlight barely making its way through the top of the stalks as we raced to our destination. I threatened to gag several times, but I did not slow with Jacob at my back and Betsie at my front.

Eventually, we broke through the sugarcane. By this time, a medium-sized crowd of slaves had congregated by the open-aired entrance of the mill which sat right next to the kogehus. Betsie, being one of the plantation's best medicine women, pushed her way to the front of the scene. Jacob and I stayed right on her tail, but I soon wished I hadn't.

A stone roller sat in front of us and a young slave I had never seen before had three-fourths of his arm stuck between it. The boy's arm was a bluish color and through the other side of the roller, I could see a small piece of sugar cane sticking out. He must have been feeding it into the roller when...this happened. Someone had given him a piece of mahoe[6] bark to bite down on. That had quieted the screams, but a mixture of tears and sweat drenched his clothes and face.

---

[6] Blue Mahoe - a type of wood native to Cuba and Jamaica; widely planted throughout the Caribbean

Briefly taking in the scene, Betsie immediately took charge. She was rattling off instructions, but they barely registered as I couldn't take my eyes off the young boy's face.

He looks terrified.

I noticed Joseph, Damien's right hand slave, taking in the scene off to my left. His face was emotionless, but his eyes were as watchful as a hawk's.

Probably so he could report back to Damien and Mr. Clark about this incident in the morning.

With that thought, my attention fell upon a man running to the back of the mill. He returned with a large axe and lined the weapon up to the visible part of the young boy's arm. Betsie held the boy, angling his head away from what was about to happen. Many of the slaves around us either bowed their heads or turned away. Bile rose up in my throat. I tried to focus on the gruesome scene, but being this close to the kogehus caused my vision to blur.

A cold sweat broke out and I faltered as my knees went weak. Noticing, Jacob reached out to steady me, but I pushed him away. I just needed some fresh air away from the crowd, so I inched my way back towards the clearing in front of the mill and kogehus. I could feel Jacob following me, but he didn't say anything and he gave me the space that I needed. With some space between me and the scene, I took in a deep breath and looked to the sky.

I can't stand there and watch what's about to happen.
He can't be more than seventeen.

The boy, whose name I had now learned was Abe, showed great strength. He did not scream when the axe came down upon his arm, but the pain must have gotten to him as two men were now carrying his unconscious body from the mill out onto the grass. When the men placed Abe in the clearing and stepped away, they revealed a boy with nothing but space on his right side from a little above his elbow on down. A small stream of blood slowly oozed from the now mostly burnt wound, but no one moved to help him further. Joseph was holding Betsie back and under his watchful eye, no one else dared budge. I knew why as soon as my eyes fell upon Jacob. The dark expression that had claimed his normally sunny face revealed the truth.

This boy won't survive.

My eyes misted over as the sheer silence overwhelmed me.

George won't be playing his banjo tune anymore tonight

Chapter 20

Eva

Blood, screams, and death haunted my dreams for eight months before some semblance of normalcy returned to me. I had plenty to keep me busy, but I couldn't stop Abe's greenish eyes from overtaking my thoughts. Since all but a small rotating group of field slaves had Sunday's off, we waited four days before burying Abe. The boy had no family left on the plantation, so Betsie and another medicine woman named Lilly prepared his body for the funeral. Although I didn't know Abe, his death hit me the hardest. For the longest time, I just couldn't escape him.

Betsie, Jacob, and I continued our dinners - they were a welcomed distraction. Sometimes, Mary would even join us as we had been spending more and more of what little free time we had together. Every day over these last eight months, Jacob left me gorgeous blue and purple flowers. He would place them on my window sill so that I returned to something beautiful each night.

"Something to make you smile and to remind you of the beauty in life," he had said after presenting the flower that first day.

It was now a Thursday afternoon. I only had a few chores to work through as Mrs. Clark was away visiting family in Wakefield, a nearby village. Last Saturday, she left behind a surprisingly short list of things for me to do in her week-long absence. Humming an old lullabye Betsie taught me, I tidied up the kitchen before heading up to the guest bedroom to sweep. Immediately, I headed to the farthest corner of the room. Instinct took over as I lost myself in the mundane sweeping motion. It was then that the hairs on my arms rose in alert. I slowly turned to find icy blue eyes locked onto my frame, the weight of *his* gaze froze me in place. Mr. Clark stalked into the room, closed the door behind him, and clicked the lock into place. I frantically rubbed at the hem of my shirt, but the action provided no comfort as Mr. Clark stepped closer. My eyes flicked towards the door.

I've got to try.

Keeping my breath even, I ducked under Mr. Clark's arm and sprinted towards the door. I had made it halfway across the room when his strong hands found me.

"I've seen the way you've been looking at me girl and I just couldn't resist your seductive ways any longer," he slurred while his left hand stroked down the side of my body.

What is he talking about?!

Using his imbalance against him, I twisted and turned with all my might, trying to break his hold. But with every struggle I made, his hands only tightened. Mr. Clark had me in a bear hug from behind. My chest struggled to inflate and slowly, my arms and legs began to feel like lead. Any and all movement felt as if I was fighting a losing battle through water. I went slack and dropped to the floor, trying to fight my way out of this, but it was too late. He had me.

"Stop....p-p-please Masta!"

Ignoring my words, he forced me up into a standing position and pressed his full body weight into me. I flinched as his lips grazed the side of my neck. His hot breath scraped across my skin as he breathed me in. I was immediately repulsed by the overwhelming smell of alcohol.

"I knew it was a good idea for Joseph to keep an eye on you," he started. His hand rose to wrap around my throat and squeezed. Mr. Clark softly pressed his lips against my right ear before continuing, "...but, I had no idea Joseph would find you with another boy, a *slave.*"

Flush against his chest, I could feel something hard poking me in my lower back. His free hand roamed down my chest. Hitting the edge of my blouse, Mr. Clark stripped the fabric off of me in one fluid motion. Although his body at my back radiated heat, I couldn't stop shivering. And while I couldn't see his face, I could hear the irritation in his voice when he spoke next.

"Joseph saw you with some boy one day, said he gave you something wrapped up through the window of *my* house. Hmmm," he breathed, "you have no idea how much I wanted to kill that boy, but Joseph said he wasn't able to get a good look at him. So, since I couldn't punish your little visitor, I knew I had to find a way to stake my claim on you - my property."

With that, Mr. Clark laid a kiss across the brand on my shoulder. His fingers soon followed, tracing the JC embedded there.

"Mine," he quietly snarled before flipping me around to face him.

His lips crashed into my unmoving ones as he backed me towards the bed. My thundering heartbeat was all I could hear as I prayed for someone, anyone to interrupt us. My hands shook at my sides as the back of my knees hit the bed frame. Mr. Clark's attack on my lips was relentless. Eventually, he forced his tongue into my mouth. Ignoring the urge to vomit, I clamped down hard on the foreign object sweeping across my teeth.

"Shit!"

Mr. Clark flew back, clutching his mouth. With a path clear, I rushed for the door, ignoring the shouts of protest coming from behind me. I had just grazed the doorknob when a sharp pain ran through my body. My feet left the ground and I went vertical as my head snapped back. Mr. Clark had his fist locked around my hair. I screamed in vain as I was dragged back. He lifted me once more and threw me onto the bed. I barely had time to blink before he was on me again, this time with his left hand pressed firmly across my mouth.

"You are not denying me this," he whispered in my ear, "I have waited long enough! I couldn't act on my feelings with my wife here. She was always getting in the way of us spending time together...making you wash late into the night. But now...she's not here and with her gone, we can finally be alone."

Mr. Clark removed his hand from my face to quickly undo the belt around his waist. Holding me down with one hand, he used the other to swiftly unfasten his slacks. A faint "click" rang out as his pants and belt slid to the floor. I wanted to scream, but every time I opened my mouth, nothing came out. His sky blue eyes held mine as his right hand darted between us. I closed my eyes and began to count.

Chapter 21

Eva

It had been six weeks since…well, you know.

My run in with Mr. Clark

I found myself looking down at the little bit of food I had managed to eat this morning. I had felt a little faint and clammy while washing dishes for Mrs. Clark earlier. I must have looked bad because just seeing my face was enough to convince Mrs. Clark to give me a sick day.

- That, and maybe a little bit of guilt for what had happened when she left -

Ever since his wife's return, Mr. Clark had become scarce once more. Although I rarely saw him, his...attack made me jumpier and quieter, especially around the Main House. The slightest movement, bump, or noise had me racing to a door or hyperventilating. I refused to put my back to another open door in the house, and I found myself glued to Mrs. Clark more than usual. She definitely picked up on my change in demeanor, but she never questioned why I asked to stay behind and wash with her for longer than usual, and, like today, she was all too happy to release me from my duties.

Getting permission to leave the Main House from Mrs. Clark, I respectfully nodded at her and sent a small smile towards a concerned Betsie watching me from the kitchen before taking my leave. I had made it a few paces away from my hut when saliva filled my mouth and my stomach flipped. Racing forward, I was only able to make it to the side of my house when everything from this morning's breakfast ended up on the grass. Taking a deep breath, I reached up and released the bandana I had tied around my hair. Dabbing it across my mouth, I slowly made my way over to a trough that was filled with some leftover rain water. The warm water still felt divine as it splashed across my face. However, the urge to vomit hit me again as I pressed my back against my hut. I slid along the wood until my butt hit the ground. Grimacing at the foul taste in my mouth, I tried my best to keep my breathing even as my insides tore themselves apart. I had just placed my head between my knees to try and find some relief when I felt a hand on my shoulder. Looking up, I found Betsie towering over me. Her almond eyes flickered between me and the disgusting pile of vomit a few paces away.

"Oh child, ya look a little worse fo' wear. Come - come on, let's get ya inside."

Grabbing me around the waste, Betsie placed one of my arms across her shoulders, steading me. Side by side, she walked me into my hut and laid me out on the mat in the corner.

"Shouldn't you be making lunch, how'd you get some time to come help me," I questioned.

"I may be a cook, but I'm also one of tha best healers they got 'round here. Masta Clark wouldn't want to unnecessarily lose one of his expensive cattle now would he?" Betise winked at me before continuing, "Seeing how slow ya moved on yo' way back to tha quarters, I asked Mrs. Clark if I could go check on ya. She agreed and Mary ended up handling lunch service wit tha help of Katy and Lilly. Plus, I thought dis would be a great time fo' us to talk since you've been awfully quiet at dinners."

Not trusting myself to speak, I just nodded in acknowledgement. Placing a wet cloth across my forehead, Betsie reached into a small satchel she kept at her side. She pulled a small root from within and placed a piece in my mouth.

"Chew on dis piece of ginger Eva - it'll help wit tha sickness."

I was filled with an overwhelming sense of deja-vu and although it felt as if my insides were dying, I couldn't help but smile.

"There's that smile. I always love seein' it...but now, why dontcha tell me how long you've been feelin' like dis?"

Moving the piece of ginger to the side of my mouth, I responded, "I've been feeling like this for the past week now. Other than today, I haven't thrown up since two days ago though. I must have a bug that's been going around. Pretty sure I saw Tess suffering from nausea last week, I most likely got it from her."

Betsie looked away in thought for a moment before taking a deep breath. She then turned back towards me and the pity I found in her eyes had my hands brushing against the ends of my shirt.

I am not going to like what's coming next.

"Eva," Betsie started. I could hear her conflicting emotions at war within the pause she took, "I hate to bring dis up, but hasn't it been a few weeks since...since what happened wit tha Masta?"

Betsie placed both of my hands in hers and clutched them to her chest. She knew this was the last thing I wanted to be discussing.

"I don't see what that has to do with this," I quietly answered. My shoulders folded in on themselves as I tried my best to disappear into the floor.

Betsie was quiet for a long time.

"B-B-Bestie, you k-k-know I hate it when y-y-you're quite like this, it m-m-makes me n-n-nervous. So whatever is on y-y-your m-m-mind, please just s-s-say it"

Betsie smiled at me knowingly before her lips turned into a grimace, "I hate to tell ya this, but Terri isn't sick she's...pregnant, her and her husband are expecting."

My stomach dropped as I realized just what Betsie was insinuating.

"Eva," Betsie tried to continue.

"No," I interrupted, "I can't be pregnant!"

"But Eva sweetie," Betsie began, "tha timeline fits and I've handled a lot of pregnancies since I've been on 'dis here plantation. Your - your symptoms are ones I normally see in those that are pregnant."

Ms. Betsie's words swarmed my head and hot saliva coated my tongue. Sensing something wrong, Betsie reached for a makeshift basket I had and held it up as I gagged into it. Placing the basket by my side, Betsie pulled me into a fierce embrace. My shoulders shook as tears began to fall. When they slid down my face and onto Betsie's arms, I felt her tighten her hold on me.

"Shhhh," Betsie said as one of her hands rubbed across my back, "It will be okay, there are things we can do."

Betsie's words failed to register as *that* day played over and over in my head.

This can't be.

Chapter 22

Eva

The next day, I was extremely jittery. I couldn't focus on my tasks and the word *pregnant* echoed throughout my head. Betsie suggested another day off, but I needed to do something with my hands. I needed to forget.

I can't give birth to his baby.

Mrs. Clark had retired to her room for a nap while I cleaned and put away some of the china. As I was making my way through the dishes, the side door closest to the kitchen smacked open. I jumped at the noise and felt the porcelain plates I was holding slip through my fingers. I stared down in horror at the blue and white pieces before footsteps forced my eyes up. Damien, the head overseer, stood before me. Now that I was seeing him in the light of day, his green eyes looked dull and his skin seemed even more red than I remembered. A deep frown graced his face as he stared down at me.

“You broke the Clark’s china girl?”

“I-I-I didn’t mean to, it’s just that y-y-you startled m-m-me -”

“Oh, so this is my fault?” Damien interrupted. Anger flashed behind his eyes as he stalked towards me.

“I-I-I’m sorry, I-I-I’ll clean it up right away.”

I bent down to collect the broken pieces, but was stopped when Damien’s hand clasped around my left wrist.

“I’ll have someone else clean this up - you, girl, need to be punished,” he spat. I flinched back as his spittle hit me in the face.

Damien gathered both of my wrists in one of his hands before dragging me back out the door he came through. I saw Mary’s head pop up in question as I was dragged past the Clark’s garden. Her eyes widened at the scene and she clutched her small digging tool to her chest before making eye contact.

"Breathe through it," she mouthed.

My heels dug into the mud as I was led to a small clearing between the slave quarters and Damien/Joseph's houses. There in the center of the clearing was a wooden platform with a post through the middle. Damien pushed me forward and I slammed into the platform. I groaned on impact before sliding into the mud. I hit with so much force that several people poked their heads out of their huts to see what was happening.

"That's right," Damien called, "come watch what happens when you mess up. *This* is why you follow orders around here!"

Damien reached down and ripped the back of my shirt open. With the back of my shirt in tatters, Damien grabbed me by the neck and led me up onto the platform. Tied to the pole in the center was a thick piece of rope. Damien unhooked it and tied my hands over one another around the pole. I was facing the slave quarters and could only watch as slave after slave reluctantly formed an audience before me. Shame and sympathy were their offerings as I was placed in position for my punishment.

"No!" someone towards the back of the crown called out.

I looked up to see Betsie, who had been visiting a sick slave, racing towards the clearing. For the first time, I saw true horror play out across her normally warm face. She rushed forward in an attempt to help, but I stopped her with a quick shake of my head.

There is nothing you can do Betsie, but get your own self in trouble.

Thankfully I didn't see Jacob, he would have been an even bigger problem. From behind me, Damien unfurled the large whip he kept at his side. The double knotted tip hit the platform with a hard "thump". Testing it, he swung it out to his right.

CRACK.

The whip made a sound like a bomb going off. Everyone, including myself, jumped at the noise. Remembering Mary's words as I passed her, I took a deep breath in. I tried to steel myself for the pain to come. I waited and waited for Damien to begin when he called out to the growing audience.

"Joseph!" he yelled.

Angling my head to the left, I could just make out Joseph, Damien's right hand slave and junior overseer. A dark-skinned woman I had often seen around clutched onto him from behind and two young children were clasped onto his legs. Handing his kids over to his wife, Joseph stepped forward, head held high. The sight was in stark contrast to most of the other slaves in attendance whose heads were angled down towards the ground.

"Here," Damien said, holding out the handle towards Joseph, "You will deliver the punishment, 50 lashes for the 5 plates she broke."

I couldn't see Damien, but I could hear the sadistic delight in his voice. Joseph didn't hesitate, nor did his face betray his feelings. Joseph strode up the platform's two steps and took the whip from Damien. Satisfied, Damien hopped off the platform to watch from a distance. As soon as Damien was out of the way, Joseph came down on my back without warning. The whip and my flesh connected with a sickening sound.

One.

I bit down into my lip and tried to breathe. I focused in on Betsie as Joseph brought the whip down again and again.

Two.

Three.

Four.

Betsie's eyes were misty and her lip quivered, but she never looked away. When the fifth lash came down, I felt the skin on my back split. Hummingbirds fluttered away from the treetops as I screamed out in agony. The sun was at its highest point and just like Joseph, it beat down on me without mercy. Tears blinded my vision as my back stung and splintered. Blood streamed out of the wounds and down my back. I could just make out the splatter pattern it made as the blood crashed to the floor. My cries didn't deter Joseph, he was relentless. I had counted to 20 when a strange numbness took over. My feet scraped across the wooden platform as my knees gave out. My arms stretched to full extension as I sagged forward, placing most of my weight against the whipping post.

Twenty-two.

Twenty-three.

Twenty-four.

A metallic taste coated the back of my throat as I gagged. My head drooped to the side and a ruby-red string of saliva slid past my lips. It dribbled onto the platform, adding a pink tint to the tears already there. Using my remaining strength, I glanced back at Joseph. Out the corner of my eye, we made eye contact and he faltered. For a split second, Joseph hesitated...but only for a moment. Sweat dripped from his brow and his chest heaved with every breath.

Why are you doing this?

That question rang through my head as the onslaught continued.

Twenty-seven.

Twenty-eight

Twenty-nine.

My eyes drifted off to the left and it was then that I made out the blurred outline of Joseph's family. His wife clutched her two children to her chest, their faces pressed into the front of her shirt. There were equal parts terror and relief in her watchful gaze. That's when it hit me.

Joseph is doing this for them. Every gruesome punishment he performs on his own people, every order he follows, means a bit more security for his family.

Understanding spread throughout my body and I couldn't help but feel sorry for Joseph. The thirtieth lash connected and my vision darkened. I welcomed the feeling. But before it could completely pull me under, I remembered my current condition.

The baby...

A strange tranquility washed over me.

If I die up here, at least I won't have to deal with my pregnancy...my child won't have to suffer.

Another lash rang out and my eyelids sagged. This time, I let the darkness take me. I remembered the thundering beat of hooves and a shout that sounded strangely like Mr. Clark before I slipped into nothing.

Chapter 23

Eva

I woke with a start and immediately begged for sleep to return as an excruciating ache rocked through me. I was laying on my stomach, my head turned towards a wooden wall. The surface couldn't have been but a mere arms length away, yet it was fuzzy and out of focus. I tried to take in a deep breath, but my back stung in protest. Groaning, I closed my eyes and focused on taking small, shallow breaths. That's when I noticed cool beads of liquid sliding down my sides. Deciding to risk the movement, I turned my head to the right as slowly as I could without disturbing another part of my body. As my head settled back down into my makeshift pillow, *my folded arms,* I came face to face with a blurry Jacob. Blinking rapidly, I forced my eyes to focus. He smirked softly at me, but I noticed his eyes were puffy and red.

"Wha- what happened," I croaked. The metallic taste from before recoated my tongue and I winced.

"Don't push yourself, take it easy...please," Jacob urged as he reached down into a pot by the bed. "Here, suck on this piece of ice. Ma went to go fetch some more for your back."

"What happened?" I tried again. My voice was hoarse, but thankfully, no blood came out that time.

"I'm sorry I wasn't there," Jacob whispered after placing a small chunk of ice between my lips.

Taking a moment, I relished in the feel of the ice melting and sliding down my throat. It soothed the dry cracks there and helped cool my mind.

"I'm glad you weren't," I countered once my mouth was clear, "There was nothing you could have done...and you know it - now what happened? The last thing I remember is getting to thirty lashes."

Jacob flinched at the number. I could tell he wanted to argue, but when I coughed hard, his whole body deflated. Taking a deep breath, he instead brought a cloth up to dab at my lips and then brushed strands of hair from my face. I subconsciously leaned into the contact as much as my back would allow.

"Well," he started, "Ma said as soon as you fainted, Mr. Clark came riding in on his horse and stopped everything. He seemed pretty angry that your back was going to be scarred up. Punished Damien and Joseph both, said five lashes would have been plenty."

A "Hmmmm," was all I could manage in response.

"As soon as Betsie was sure the beating was over, she rushed to you. Two slaves in the audience helped carry you back to your hut. Ma and I have been fussing over you ever since. Definitely gave us a scare," Jacob's eyes fell to the ground and his right hand began to shake, "you've been in and out of consciousness for two days."

"Two days!?" I exclaimed, lifting up slightly. My body quickly reminded me why moving was a terrible idea. Wincing, I slowly laid back down. "Can you help turn me on my side, my stomach needs a break?"

"I told you to take it easy," Jacob remarked as he helped guide me into a comfortable position.

I could feel my back stretch unnaturally. My hands clenched together at the prickling feeling, but I was able to breathe a little easier on my side.

"If it's been two days, what are you doing here. Aren't you missing your duties?" I questioned.

"I feigned being sick so that I could come check up on you. I had to be here in case you woke up."

"If Mr. Clark finds out you came to visit me, he just might continue what Joseph and Damien started - but this time on both us," a short laugh escaped my lips.

Unamused, Jacob refused to answer. Instead, he pushed the stool he was sitting on closer to my mat and placed his hands on either side of my slightly round stomach. Even through the fabric of the thin sheet that covered me, his hand's warmth burned. Normally the touch would have sent my heart soaring, but instead my stomach dropped and I snapped my eyes shut for fear of vomiting.

"It's still there, isn't it?"

As if hearing my question, my stomach swirled and something thumped against Jacob's hand.

"Well I think that answers your question," Jacob breathed. Although he tried to hide it, I watched as wonder and awe flashed across his face.

Looking up at me, he composed himself and smirked in an attempt to lighten the mood, but my frown only deepened. His hands dropped from my sides and for a while, only silence passed between us.

"Do you want to keep it?"

He spoke so quietly, his question barely registered. Looking up at him, my eyebrows scrunched up in uncertainty, "What do you mean?"

"My mother has performed things in the past, things that...make sure the baby does not survive. This…this is an option if you want it."

Unable to look directly at him, I instead followed the mesmerizing flight pattern of a fly making its way through my hut. Sensing my discomfort, his hands came up to my face, forcing me to look at him.

"Whatever you choose, just know I'll ha-, ma and I will have your back."

An answer to his earlier inquiry rang loud in my head, but refused to escape my lips:

I don't know… I don't know if I want it.

Chapter 24

Eva

It had been a month since the lashing and with each passing day, the scars on my back slowly turned a dull greyish color.

They kind of mirror Jacob's almost.

Betsie told me the change in color means I'm healing properly - she was worried they were going to stay puffy and pink. All I had to say about them was that I was glad to be rid of the constant pain. A sharp pain might have shot up my back occasionally when I reached for something or over stretched while washing or cleaning. But thankfully, nothing came close to the discomfort I felt after those first two weeks.

It was a Sunday and Betsie and I went on an errand to kill two birds with one stone. Mrs. Clark needed some beauty items and I...

"Needed to have a well deserved break," as Betsie had put it.

Thus, we found ourselves sitting side by side, gossiping ferociously on our way to a market in the city. A few other slave women completed the group. We were all pressed into the back of a wagon, the canvas tent around us flapped as we bounced along the road. The same slave from my first days here drove it. He wouldn't be shopping with us, but was ready to load anything the Clark's needed onto it to carry back to the plantation. Against my will, my right leg began to jiggle in excitement. I had only been able to visit the market a handful of times in my year and half on the Clark plantation, and each time I went I was awed by the sights and smells.

This is definitely what I needed.

The sun had fully risen when the wagon rolled to a stop. Jumping out first, I offered my hand to Betsie and some of the other women as they exited. There were booths set up every five paces. Men and women were engaged in all sorts of conversations as vendors sold any and everything out of carts or storefronts. The smell of fresh bread made my mouth water as we walked past a stone oven. Betsie and I stopped to stand in its warmth before continuing on.

More rejuvenating than the sun.

Women of all backgrounds were also about. Women of high stature, women of low-stature, ladies with fair skin, pale skin, dark skin, and even light, caramel brown skin were in attendance. A group of the latter gossiped in a corner. Their skin mirrored mine, but they wore the finest gowns I had ever seen. Their matching umbrellas provided additional shade as they laughed. From afar, I admired the various colored jewels sparkling around their necks.

Betsie tugged on my arm and led me to a small open plaza. People lounged and bustled, the market thrummed with an energy I had been missing since leaving Cuba. Another group of women, in less ostentatious gowns, escorted men off of the dirt roads and into a tavern. The smell of rum and their laughter wafted out of the building and mingled with the sea-salted air. Betsie and I shared a smile before she pulled me over to our favorite booth. A man named Carlos worked it and his face lit up as soon as he saw us. I didn't really know Carlos' true age, but I figured he had to be about 40 or 50. He was tanned to a golden brown, bald, and when he smiled, little lines formed at the corners of his eyes. Betsie had known him for years, seven according to her, and everytime we came to the market, we made sure to stop by and say hello. He knew some of the best jokes, jokes that would make your belly ache in elation. He would even throw an orange our way in return for our company. This time was no different. Piercing the hard flesh, Betsie and I split the orange down the middle and leisurely snacked on pieces as we made our way through the list Mrs. Clark gave us. The sun had moved half past twelve before we acquired everything needed. Searching for items was exciting and peaceful. By the time we were done, my heart, mind, and steps felt a little bit lighter. I had been wary of going out with Betsie this soon after my ordeal, but the trip had been a welcomed distraction.

As Betsie and I were leaving town with everything Mrs. Clark requested, we passed through a grand stone archway. Halfway through it, something fluttered along the outskirts of my vision. Turning towards the movement, a single piece of tattered parchment caught my eye. The word "WANTED" was plastered at the top in bold lettering. Pausing in front of it, recognition and understanding hit me as I read the poster:

"Hercules, wanted dead or alive. His crimes include: kidnapping slaves, stealing provisions, and burning and raiding plantations."

That's the name Mrs. Clark mentioned all those months ago.

"Betsie," I called, "do you know of this man?"

Making her way over to me, Betsie glanced at the crude image of a dark skinned man on the page. His eyes were piercing and his face had been printed with a scowl.

"What does it say?" Betsie asked.

"People are looking for a man named Hercules."

At the mention of his name, Betsie quickly scanned our surroundings. We were alone save for a couple other slave women making their way back to the wagon. Betsie stepped closer to me and lowered her voice.

"I always thought he was a ghost, but I have heard talk amongst some of tha slaves about a resistance. Whispers of free communities within tha trees - apparently, Hercules is a leader of one of them."

“I heard mistress Clark mention him before as well - apparently he’s causing issues for Mr. Clark. Might have been responsible for the crop burning we had months ago.” Now it was my turn to quickly survey our surroundings, “I never mentioned this, but I found a note on Mr. Clark's Desk. Damien and some of the other workers were searching for the person who burned the fields, but they never found him.”

My blood warmed and my heartbeat quickened as my brain worked to put all the pieces together.

“We have to tell Jacob about this,” I fiercely whispered.

Betsie considered me carefully. She took a deep breath and when she spoke, she sounded weary: “Ya can let him know suga, but if ya ask me, it sounds too good to be true.”

Chapter 25

Eva

Night had long since arrived by the time we got back to the plantation. My body had been thrumming with energy ever since finding the wanted ad. I couldn't shake the pressure that bloomed in my chest.

If there's merit to this Hercules, we could change everything.

As soon as we had dropped off our purchases at the Main House, I dragged Betsie to Jacob's and called a family meeting. I forgot how to breathe as I recounted everything I had learned: from overhearing Mr. and Mrs. Clark's argument, to the discovery I made in Mr. Clark's study, to the Hercules poster at the market. Jacob and Betsie wore the same expression as they listened to me. But as soon as I was done, Jacob broke character and leapt to his feet.

“See I told you mom,” he began, whispering under his breath as he paced. “I’ve also been hearing things, little stories shared between some of the sugar cane workers. There’s talk of joining these slave communities...we can escape to the hills. Eva can escape Masta Clark and we can-”

Betsie had been deathly quiet up until that point, but she interrupted her son’s impassioned speech with a thump of her fist against the wall - “we can what?” she questioned.

She did not yell, but the fury in her voice was palpable. It wrapped itself around my nerves and I shivered, “What would ya have us do - risk escapin’ to sum unknown place? A place that may or may not exist, and then what,” Betsie paused to look her son dead in the face, “we get caught, strung up, and beaten. I can’t watch ya go through that again - either of ya. Eva has been through enough. You have been through enough. We should just keep our heads down an-”

“Die slaves mama? That’s not a life!” Jacob tried to grasp his mother, to steady her, but she shrugged him off.

Pinching the bridge of her nose, Betsie countered, “I’d rather take a life of certainty in bondage than risk everything on fairy tales and ghost stories.”

Her words hung in the air like smoke, choking any dreams that dared rise. For the first time ever, Betsie turned her back on us and stormed out in a fit of anger. Jacob’s door rattled with the force of her leave. A heavy emptiness took over the hut in her absence. It consumed us, and Jacob and I could only stare at one another in disbelief.

Chapter 26

Eva

Things were tense between Jacob and Betsie for a few weeks. Jacob even stopped coming to a couple of dinners, but after knocking some sense into him one night, he put his pride aside and came back round. Mary was surprisingly a big help in that conversation.

"She's still your mother," Mary had softly remarked the night we staged our intervention. Those words and the way she bore into Jacob with her wide, bright eyes were what eventually convinced him to relent.

At least, that's what I thought.

With Jacob and Betsie back on speaking terms, weekly dinners were better than ever. Jacob nor I dared mention Hercules again, at least not in Betsie's presence, and Mary worked as a wonderful buffer. We slipped back into a sem-comfortable bliss, as comfortable as we could get on a sugar plantation. Two months later though, things got even better.

Or so we had thought.

A month after Betsie's and I's trip to the market, Mrs. Clark announced that she and her husband would be moving back to England. All of the house slaves in attendance shuffled restlessly as we all thought the same thing.

She's going to ask some of us to accompany her back home.

We were shocked when she instead revealed a proxy overseer would be left in charge of the plantation in their absence.

Whatever that means.

Some of the women next to me breathed sighs of relief. I on the other hand was conflicted. Flicking my eyes towards her, I found Mrs. Clark looking in my direction as well. We made eye contact for a fleeting moment before my head dropped down into a low nod. My hands grasped at the sides of my dress and my stomach clenched. I had gotten used to Mrs. Clark. There was more to her than met the eye and although she could be ruthless and mean, she was the devil I knew.

This new overseer would be an unknown.

A month had passed since Mrs. Clark's announcement and all of the house slaves were spread out along the Main House's front steps. We created a walkway from the house to a carriage waiting in the roundabout at the base of the property. A handful of field workers who were currently off shift were also in attendance. They formed a small crowd to the right of the carriage. I could see silent cheers going off in several of the house slaves' heads as we watched Damien, Mr. Clark, and Mrs. Clark descend the stairs between us. No matter how mixed my feelings were for Mrs. Clark, I sent up a silent prayer of thanks that Damien and Mr. Clark would soon be gone. When the former passed by me, I felt an overwhelming urge to spit. But, my neutral demeanor didn't threaten to crack until Mr. Clark stopped right in front of me. I refused to meet his eyes, instead I looked straight ahead and past him. After a moment though, one of his hands reached up to gently stroke my cheek. Biting down hard on my tongue, I resisted the urge to run.

Peace Eva - after a few minutes, you will never have to see him again .

The moment between us lasted far too long. But eventually Mrs. Clark nudged her husband forward. She did not acknowledge me. When they reached the bottom of the stairs, the trio climbed into the wagon and were off. When the dust from their departure cleared, the new overseer emerged from the Main House. He was stoic, tall, lanky, and had the slightest of grins as he watched the Clarks leave.

Chapter 27

Eva

With the installation of a new man in charge, many things changed. The overseer, Eric, was young and unmarried. Thus, he had little use for house slaves. All we had to tend to was the cooking of his meals and the upkeep of the house and garden. This left Betsie, Mary, and I with much more free time than usual. Although us house workers saw an ease in our schedules, those who worked the fields weren't as lucky. Sugar production went into overtime under Eric's management, leading to more frequent illnesses, injuries, and deaths. As a result, Betsie, Mary, and I normally spent our free time aiding the field workers in any way possible. We tried our best to make sure they had water and food, and came running whenever there was need for a healer. Despite this rampant increase in the sugar production schedule, things were relatively quiet…for all of two weeks at least. That's when the unthinkable happened.

I was in the basement of the Main House making my way through Eric's small pile of laundry when a series of muffled cries rang out. Wiping my wet hands across the front of my dress, I lept to my feet and ran up the stairs. Knowing that Betsie and Mary were preparing Eric's lunch, I rushed to them first to see if they knew what was going on. However, when I entered the kitchen, the room was empty. Half-made food littered the countertops and an orange liquid covered the floor. That's when a louder scream met my ears, followed by two yells of protest. My eyes bulged and my heart dropped to the floor as I recognized one of the shouts.

Betsie.

I rushed through the kitchen's side door and was floored by the scene in front of me. Mary and another house worker, Tess, were laid out in the dirt clutching their sides. Eric had his hand wrapped around Betsie's throat, her normally bright eyes were red and splotchy.

"You tried to poison me!" Eric's voice boomed as he flung Betsie to the ground.

"No sir, I swear I wasn't tryin' to poison ya, I-I-I just didn't know ya was allerg-"

WHAP.

Eric backhanded Betsie, stopping her mid sentence. I watched in horror as blood seeped from the corner of her mouth. My hands shook with the familiarity of that moment.

"You think I'm going to believe a word you say, I know you tried to poison me!" Eric spat.

He closed his hand into a fist and swung back, ready to strike Betsie again. I made eye contact with Mary. She swiftly shook her head no, but fear (and love) made me stupid. In a split second, I sprinted towards Eric, throwing myself between him and Betsie. His fist collided with the back of my shoulder, right above the brand. The combined force of my lunge and the punch rocked me into the dirt. Shaking the stars from my eyes, I crawled to a kneeling position in front of Betsie.

"Please," I begged. My breath came hard and fast as I reached behind me and grabbed on to Betsie's leg. "She worked for the Clark's for 8 years without incident...She'd never poison you."

Ignoring me, Eric stepped forward, pushed me out of the way, and snatched Betsie up by the arms. I willed my mind to think of something, anything, to get Eric to stop.

"Masta Eric please, Betsie's the best healer you have on this plantation, please d-d-d-on't punish her."

"Everyone can be replaced," he answered without looking back.

I sucked in a breath as panic set in. Whipping my head around, I addressed

Mary as quietly as I could, "Find Jacob - now."

Her wide eyes held tears and her hands trembled, but she picked herself up off the floor, grabbed Tess, and ran towards the slave quarters. Turning around, I took off after Betsie and Eric. Scrapes were now visible all up and down Betsie's legs. She thrashed and pleaded, but it fell upon death ears. Eric was slowly making his way towards the whipping post. I could just make out dark brown spots along the platform's surface where my own blood had dried.

They had just made it to the edge of the whipping post when Betsie was able to wrangle an arm free. Eric faltered in surprise, giving Betsie enough room to run. She sprinted towards me, tears were streaming down her face. Our fingertips had barely brushed when her head snapped back. Eric had caught up and had Betsie by her hair.

That move had been done on me before, but it was something else entirely to have to watch it be done to someone you love.

I dropped to my knees and when she called out in pain, I flinched - it was a pain I knew all too well. With a deep scowl, Eric shoved Betsie back towards the platform. Something he didn't account for was the mud. Betsie stumbled back three steps before tripping. Her body twisted sideways and her hands struggled to get out in front of her. A silent scream ripped through me as the world seemed to slow. Everything lagged and I couldn't seem to move fast enough. All I could do was watch as Betsie fell back, her head colliding with the corner of the platform. A sickening crack reverberated through me.

"Look at what you did to yourself," Eric spat in disgust.

But Betsie didn't respond, she didn't move.

The mud in the pit that had formed around the whipping post sloshed as I rushed over. I slid to a stop beside her and everything else in the world blocked out. She was turned away from me. Mud coated us both as I knelt behind her and softly placed a hand on her shoulder. She did not respond to my touch. With my hands unsteady, I increased my hold on Betsie and rolled her over into my lap. Her head lolled against my chest, but her eyes were wide open. Immediately, a sticky and warm fluid gushed out over me.

Blood?

It oozed from a large gash at the side of her head. Her body was still warm, but there was nothing behind her eyes. No light, no joy, nothing.

"Betsie?" my voice quivered.

A single tear streaked down my face as I placed a wobbling hand to her chest. A movement I had seen Betsie do time and time again.

One.

Two.

Please Betsie.

Three.

I held my breath and waited, but there was no thump of her heart.

She was gone.

“No,” a sob that had been building rocked through me as I surrounded Betsie’s body with mine.

After five minutes, I became vaguely aware of a male presence to my left. Instincts had me shielding Betise’s body away from the intruder. But when I looked up through my blurred vision, Jacob was at my side. He dropped to his knees and collapsed over us. I had never seen him shed one tear, but that day, his cries echoed throughout the whole plantation.

Chapter 28

Eva

I had refused to leave Betsie's body until we buried her two days later. I slept by her side, ate by her side, and prayed for a strength I didn't think I had. I knew it was a risk, but I didn't care what Eric did to me - I just couldn't abandon her. Surprisingly though, Eric never commented on my absence. With Betsie gone, the preparation of her body fell upon me and Lilly, another healer. The work provided me with the perfect distraction. I wasn't able to dwell on my sorrow as I tried my best to put together an incredible memorial.

It has to reflect who she was and the gaping hole she's leaving behind.

Jacob was scarce leading up to her funeral, but I attributed it to his grief. Things didn't feel off until he failed to show up the day of her burial. Several times throughout the service, I found myself searching him out only to feel the heavy weight of disappointment. Then, a week went by without seeing him. I would stop by his hut before starting and after finishing my duties, but I always found it dark. I questioned Mary, George, and many of the field workers, but no one could attest to his whereabouts. His disappearance had everything on this grand plantation feeling way too small. I became frantic as a week turned into two and then three. That's when the truth sank in.

He left me.

I wanted to be mad, wanted to curse his name into the night, but no matter how frustrated or angry I got, I couldn't slander him. Mostly because I was truly mad at myself. I went against my better judgement. I took a chance and decided to open my heart to him and his mother. And now my worst fear, the very thing I had wanted to avoid when I first came here, had come true. Also, how could I fault Jacob for taking his chance at freedom after everything that had happened.

...what did I expect, for us to be a family?

That third week after Jacob's disappearance, I was walking back to the slave quarters after an unusually long list of tasks. I trudged through the humid night air feeling like half of my former self. Everything seemed dull, and the dark circles under my eyes were in stark contrast with the rest of my skin. The grass crunched under my feet as I made the long trek back to my hut. I could faintly hear George's workday song in the distance, but that day I glowered at the lilty melody. All it did was remind me of conversations and moments now long gone. My feet moved on autopilot, as I lost myself to thought. But when I finally came to a stop, my hut didn't stand before me. Instead, a structure with a sun etched deep into the wood took up my field of vision. Locking in on the sun, my body began to shake and everything I had been holding in over the last few weeks came flooding out. My chest felt hollow and ached as my knees collided with the ground. Placing my hands in front of me, and my head on top of them, I begged to be free of the memories that plagued my mind. Each one was like a dagger through my heart.

Chapter 29

Eva

Four weeks after Jacob's disappearance, I found myself startled awake by the thick smell of burning oak. Coughing, I jumped up from my mat and stayed low to the ground as I made my way to the door. Smoke filtered in through the window to the right of it, coating my room in a hazy fog. My eyes burned, but I stayed quiet and pressed my ear up against the door. I slowed my breathing in an attempt to hear screams or anything else that might be going on outside. Instead, a jaring shiver ran through me.

...nothing, I hear nothing

That was until two strong, solid knocks vibrated through the door and my bones. My knees cracked as I slowly rose from the floor. I placed my hand against the door frame and briefly closed my eyes as I made my ascent.

One,

Two,

Three...

Cracking the door open a few inches, a sliver of bright orange light assaulted my eyes. Blinking, I tried to restore my vision before something large blocked everything out.

"Are you Eva Turner?" - The body in front of me rumbled.

His accent threw me off. It was exaggerated and his r's seemed to roll from his mouth. Pulling the door fully open, I stood face to chest with a stoic man. He was dressed in a loose white v-neck shirt and a pair of tan breeches that came just below the knee. His torso was wider than the door frame.

"Eva Turner?" The man repeated.

Finding my voice, I quickly stuttered, "yes."

Despite my erratic heartbeat, I wasn't afraid of the stranger. Tilting my head up, I peered into his midnight face. Upon closer inspection, my eyebrows arched up in surprise.

I know this man!

Before he could speak again, his name surged past my lips.

"Hercules?"

The man from the posters around town, the mythical man of a seemingly unattainable future now stood before me. Although he definitely shouldn't be here, he didn't seem to be in a rush. At the mention of his name however, I noticed him straighten.

"That is my name, I have come to find you - Jacob sent me."

At the mention of Jacob, my heart lurched. Suddenly, the room began to spin and I faltered, reaching out for purchase that wasn't there. Stepping forward with an uncanny speed, Hercules grabbed me before my feet gave out completely. Once I was stable again, he gently released me and took a step back towards the door.

"You know Jacob?" That was the only coherent thought I could voice.

"Yes," he tersely replied, " and you need to come with me now."

The latter half of his statement fell upon death ears.

"How...how do you know of Jacob?"

Hercules' eyes narrowed in frustration. I could tell he wanted to move on from this topic as his jaw clenched. However, after a small beat, his nostrils flared and he released a long breath through them before speaking.

"Jacob found his way to our community some days ago - told me that this plantation had to be the next liberation sight. I had been targeting this plantation already on smaller missions but he said that with the main owners gone, this was the perfect time to take the plantation completely. I was asked to find you personally," he spoke quickly. Glancing back out the door, he added, "Miss Eva, we really need to go now." His words were soft yet forceful as he stepped to the side and gestured to my bed. "Gather your things quickly."

My throat constricted as I swept my eyes around my hut. There wasn't much to grab because...

This isn't my home.

Coughing hard, my attention was drawn back to the smoke wafting through the air. Now that Hercules had moved, I could finally see outside. Sugar cane as far as I could see was on fire. The burning stalks tinted the sky a bright orange and added about twenty more degrees to the already humid weather. The sugar cane crackled and hissed, rebelling loudly against the normally quiet night. The sugar cane roared as it was consumed by heat, as if finally voicing its discontent at all the horrors it had witnessed. As the smoke rose toward the sky, I saw the faces of the ones these fields had claimed. Abe, William, Thomas, Grace, Abigail. There were countless ghostly forms and worst of all, in front of them all, was Betsie. Just the thought of her sent waves of anger as hot as the fire outside through me.

These are the faces of those I'd be leaving behind...I'd be leaving her behind.

But as I forced myself to look into the rippling face of Betsie, I found no traces of pain. Her eyes shifted and swirled, but they were just as bright as always. As she peered into me, an overwhelming sense of peace washed over me, and in that moment, I knew she would never truly be far from my heart. As the smokey forms of Betsie and a fraction of those we'd lost dissipated, I blinked, finally taking note of everything else happening outside my door. Shockingly, in front of those burning stalks stood hundreds of Clark Plantation workers. They made a semi circle around the outside of my hut and the crowd was steadily growing. There were some faces I didn't recognize, but Mary's stood out immediately. A rare smile graced her face as we made eye contact. She clutched at the black sack tied around her back.

Seeing Mary's face knocked me out of my daze. With no further hesitation, I threw my few pieces of clothing and two hand-made gourd cups onto my bed sheet. Grabbing the ends and fastening them into a double knot, I nodded at Hercules who had made his way back outside. His hand was outstretched, ready to help me across the threshold. I looked around my hut one last time, took a deep breath, and strode past him into the night.

Chapter 30

Eva

[Seven Years Later]

With Jacob close behind me, I clutch the hand of the little six year old next to me, his sky blue eyes in stark contrast with the brown tint of his skin. My chest expands fully with the light and airy feeling of the day. The mountains that enclose our village funnel in a slight breeze. It dances across my skin as I bask in the sunlight. Most of the community is up and about in the midst of a wealth of activities. Everyone here has a job and a purpose, and we are free to choose what that position is. Earlier in the day, the hunters traversed further up into the mountains to find wild hogs, berries, and anything else edible. Other members are in the process of making salt necessary for meat preservation, while some clean and prepare our fertile grounds for the upcoming plant of crops. Crops that will include plantains, sweet corn, bananas, cacao, pineapples, and cassava to name a few. Along with the normal buzz of maroon life, there is an added sense of excitement in the air. Something that has my skin tingling in anticipation. Several of our maroon community's people stand with me. We have taken a break from our daily routines to now watch Hercules ride off to meet Cudjoe, one of the maroon leaders. I am told they will be discussing terms of peace with the British. A treaty is apparently involved, one that will allow us to live without fear in exchange for our help in the future against other colonial powers.

Who knows what the future will entail, but as I look down into the eyes of my child, I see love, not the malice of his father, and for the first time…hope.

THE END

Glossary

[1] “Braff” - patois for “showing off”
[2] “Kibba yuh mouth” - patois for “shut-up”
[3] “Put clothes pon yuh argument” - patois for "mind what you’re saying” or “show some respect while speaking to me”
[4] Tap - patois for “stop”
[5] The gang system was a system of division of labor within slavery on a plantation. The third gang typically encompassed the weakest workers and were given the easiest work.
[6] Blue Mahoe - a type of wood native to Cuba and Jamaica; widely planted throughout the Caribbean

Acknowledgement

I would like to thank my brother, Ronson Holmes, and my parents, Ronald Holmes and Dr. Karen Perkins-Holmes, for their unwavering support throughout my writing journey. In addition, thank you to my cousin, Shalease Allen, for her creative work on the cover of this book. I love you all tremendously.

About The Author

Kayla A. Holmes

Kayla Holmes is a young adult working in the Media and Entertainment industry. She's a creator, writer, event planner, and gamer. Originally from Owings Mills, Maryland, she graduated from The University of Pennsylvania in 2020 with a degree in Economics and minors in History and Native American Studies. It was there that the idea for this book was born. In addition to her love for History and writing, she also enjoys making people laugh. Something that's evident in her YouTube channel KayRVideos.

Printed in the USA
CPSIA information can be obtained
at www.ICGtesting.com
LVHW012142120324
774320LV00036B/1058

9 781736 967928